Ride a Wild Horse

Ride a Wild Horse

RUTH CHRISTOFFER CARLSEN

Illustrated by Beth and Joe Krush

1970 HOUGHTON MIFFLIN COMPANY BOSTON

Also by

RUTH CHRISTOFFER CARLSEN

Henrietta Goes West
Hildy and the Cuckoo Clock
Monty and the Tree House
Mr. Pudgins
Sam Bottleby

1690329

For my daughter, KRISTIN
Who remembers other worlds

CONTENTS

Ride a Wild Horse

1 Our Family Grows by One

"**I** REALLY don't care much whether you like the idea or not. It's settled."

That was my Mom talking . . . shouting might be a better description. "Being an only child has made you spoiled and selfish. It's high time you learned to consider others. Julie is coming to live with us and that's that. Barney Sutton, will you stop eating for a few minutes and listen to me?"

"I am listening," I said. I don't know how she figured I could do much else when she was almost talking in my ear. I reached for the Hydrox cookies and poured some more milk. We were standing in our big country kitchen. I always head for the kitchen the minute I hit home. I just plain like to eat . . . mainly because eating is about the only thing I do especially well. I can put away mountains of food and enjoy every minute of it.

"Barney! You are not to eat another thing before dinner. Here, give me those cookies."

I didn't have a chance to give the package to her. She about snatched it from me. Aw well, what could you expect. Mom is an awful nag. It's fuss about this and stew about that till I almost go bats. Sometimes I can ignore her, but not today. There was tension in the air. The thought hit me that Dad had probably reacted about the same way I had. Why a girl? I lumbered off to my room upstairs. One thing about eating all the time is that you're bound to get fat.

What a drag. What a drag! I threw my sweat shirt onto the top bunk bed and dived into the closet for my hidden box of Ritz crackers and the jar of peanut butter. Man! I had lots of thinking to do and it went better with food. How could Mom go off the deep end like this and take in a stranger? Okay, so the kid is about my age. I'm twelve and they thought Julie was about that age too. But to pick a girl . . . how could they be so dense as to pick a girl? When I asked that question, Mom said straight out that she and Dad thought I needed humanizing. I felt maybe they could do with a bit of humanizing themselves. Like thinking about me, really thinking about me for a change. I couldn't think of a thing that had grabbed my enthusiasm lately that somehow they hadn't instantly disregarded. Not on purpose. They aren't mean. But they never consider me when a decision's being made.

Okay, like what? Like I had learned to body surf when we lived near the ocean in Florida. Kids in the North think sliding a great sport, but you've never known real excitement till you stand out, way out in the ocean and catch a wave and ride in on it. You can zap along at thirty miles an hour. Makes you feel king of the wind. I was just getting good at it and believe me, it takes practice. So what happens? Dad changes jobs. Takes one in Iowa. You can sure bet your last wooden nickel that there's no surfing in Iowa.

Still, I couldn't object to the neighborhood we landed in. It was a good one. I don't mean ritzy or super style. I mean there were plenty of kids my age. Being fat, you take lots of ribbing and you're supposed to be funny. Okay, I'm funny. I don't threaten anyone and I make friends easily. So what does Mom do next? She finds a house way out in the country that she talks Dad into buying. I am many things, but a country boy I am not. Ugh! Gravel roads, fields of corn, smells of the barnyard. You can have 'em all.

Is it any wonder that I took to eating more and more? But this last decision was too much. To bring a girl into our family . . . a stray at that. A kid had turned up at the police station, not knowing who she was or where she had come from. I've heard of amnesia but in a twelve-year-old it doesn't make sense. She had to be up to something. Maybe she was a spy or a criminal or just a nut. None of the choices looked good. That thought made me uneasy. Even my stomach felt uneasy. That would tie it . . . If I got sick now, Mom would be sure I'd done it on purpose. Maybe I had. I lay down on the bed and dozed off. The day was a warm one for June and just walking down to the lake had tired me out. I blanked out until I heard the sound of the car. Must be Dad coming home . . . Dad and what's-her-name, my new little playmate.

I took my time getting downstairs. Mom had already gone out on the porch. We have an old-fashioned white house with a porch across the front and great gables rearing in the front and back. I had the bedroom under one gable and I suppose Julie would now have the other one. Mom and Dad's room was a huge one that ran between these two. I didn't go outside. I stood in the window staring at the car, waiting.

Jumping Jehoshaphat! here they came. First Dad — he's almost white haired, slight in build, a little stooped. Being a professor of English, he spends more time with books than exercise. And walking along behind him was the girl. She was an odd one all right. Her hair was black — jet black — and cut with square bangs and squared off sides. She was small. They were way off, whoever had figured her age. She couldn't be more than eight or nine. Her eyes looked slanty and wild. Everything about her oozed a sense of wildness. My heart gave a skip. Hey, this was going to be awful. That little kid could make my life miserable and the way she looked, I could bet she'd try.

I saw Mom step forward and shake her hand. Mom's big and rangy. She and Dad always look like the long and short of it. They're the long and short of it in lots of things. Dad's long on reading, Mom on practicality; Dad's long on dreams, Mom on plans for the day. Don't get me wrong. My Mom's plenty smart. Like now. She didn't hug and kiss and half smother this strange kid. She treated her with dignity, which was probably a good thing. I wouldn't have put it past the girl to bite or kick anyone who annoyed her.

"Barney. Barney. Julie's here," called Mom.

There was no putting it off. I had to meet her. I went to the front door, stepped outside and held my pudgy paw in her direction. Julie looked at me, right at me, and for a minute I had a strange dizzy feeling looking at her eyes. I don't remember ever looking into a girl's eyes before. The experience shook me . . . scared me.

"I am pleased to meet you, Barney Sutton," she said. Her voice was whispery. I wanted to tell her to speak up. Instead I leaned a bit toward her. "Your size is somewhat overwhelming if not repulsive. You are fat, Barney."

How's that for openers. Of course, I know I'm fat.

Because I am fat. But I hate being told right out by a stranger that I'm fat. It shrivels up my good feelings. "So what's with you?" I asked. "You think I'm so dumb I don't know I'm fat?"

"Oh," she said and her yellowish eyes . . . hey, that's queer . . . her eyes *are* yellow in color. Both the iris and pupil seemed to get larger at once, but that's impossible. "If you know you are fat," she said, "then you can do something, can't you?"

And she walked past me into the house. What absolutely devastated me was to catch Dad winking at Mom. They thought it was funny. "She's a nut," I said darkly. "You'll see. She's a real nut and we'll all be murdered in our beds."

I stomped into the house, banging the screen door loudly because Mom hates having doors slammed. And there was Julie, sitting on the sofa, her feet crossed at the ankles, her hands folded in her lap. She sure didn't act like any girl I'd ever seen before. She acted like a grown-up person in a young kid's body. And I began to wonder if this could be true. Maybe that's why she was so odd. Imagine any adult you can think of trapped in a kid's body. The idea shook me. I felt this overwhelming need for food and headed for the kitchen and the cookie jar. But I never made it.

"Barney," said Mom, "I'm going to finish dinner. Why don't you and Julie get acquainted? Simon [that's my Dad's name] Simon, dear, could you put Julie's bag in the front room? I'll take her up later and help her get settled."

And with that, both of them left. Jumping Jehoshaphat! they'd done it — they'd gone off and left me with this wild one. I sat down rather gingerly on the edge of a chair and balanced there. Neither one of us spoke. We sat. Then we sat some more. I shifted my position and glanced toward Julie. She had her eyes shut, but she didn't look as if she were sleeping — no, nor resting either. There was some kind of pent-up excitement vibrating through her. She'd never miss me. I might as well hunt for something to eat.

I started off toward the stairs. There came that whispery voice again. "You will stay, please," it said. "Your mother told you to stay."

I stopped as if my feet were pinned to the rug. This kid had charming manners. If she got any more charming I was going to kill her. I hadn't felt such anger in years . . . deep, burning, non-thinking anger. "I don't do everything my mother says. You think I'm some kind of baby or something?"

"I do not know for sure." She looked at me, studying me. "Yes, I almost think you are some kind of baby. You do not act in a mature way. You are like a great mass of trembling jelly. Push in and you let out a shriek of hurt feelings."

"Keep talking," I said, nasty like.

"I have need of a friend. Friends help each other. I need help. You need help."

"I need help." I yelled those words. "So's your Aunt Fanny. I'm perfectly okay as I am. Who says I need help? My Mom? My Dad?" I felt betrayed.

"No, no! Your mama and papa say nothing about you. The vibrations say you need help. So we will be friends. You help me and I'll help you."

She had it all planned out. I kind of shook my head. "That's not the way you make friends," I said. "Don't you know anything?"

"But that is the way we make friends where I come from," whispered Julie. "We meet someone and we recognize a friend."

"Where do you come from?" I turned and looked at her. "I thought the social worker told Mom that you didn't know where you came from?"

"I never said I didn't know. That would be lying. I simply did not tell them, because I was taught that if one miscalculated on a trip, one must be careful."

I backed up to the chair and sat down. I think better sitting. "You have been taught on trips to be careful? Has this happened to you before?"

"No, no. But we know it can happen. After we have passed through the early levels of knowledge and are deemed ready for trips, we learn first of all that something can go wrong."

I sat staring at her. She was saying plain English words but they didn't make sense. I'd never heard of levels of knowledge. Kids pass from grade to grade in any state I've lived in. But maybe in some other country . . . Maybe they did things differently, if what Julie was saying was true.

"If you're from some other country," I said slowly, thinking out loud, "how come you speak English so well? You don't even have an accent."

"I can assure you, Barney, that I am from another country," said Julie. "That is the truth."

"Okay then, why didn't you talk to them the first night? They said you didn't say one single word for three whole days," I said. "And then you talked up a storm. No hesitancy. I bet it was a trick."

"No trick," said Julie. "It takes at least three days to learn a language . . . at least for me. I am not as proficient as some in my land."

"Three days?" I leaned back in the chair, jolted to my toes. "You're telling me that you never spoke a word of English till you landed at the police station?"

"That is correct. I had to listen and listen carefully to learn the vocabulary, the sentence patterns, your usage."

"I don't believe it." I was grinding my teeth. Grinding my teeth helped me hold on to reality and I needed a firm grasp at this minute. I knew that no one, absolutely no one could learn to speak a language in three days. Only Julie said she had and for some dumb reason, I believed her.

"Do I speak correctly?" she asked.

"You speak like you swallowed a dictionary," I said. "Like no kid I've ever heard."

"So, that would be logical. I was never with . . . with kids. I was only with adults. I speak as they spoke. But now that I live here with you, I will learn . . . from you."

"I'm not much of a teacher," I muttered, feeling uneasy.

"But that does not matter. I do not want a teacher. I need only to listen. I will listen to you. And you will talk."

How about that? She had it all neatly planned out. And I didn't seem to have any choice.

"You have a barn," she said. "That is correct?"

"We have a barn but it's not been used as a barn for ages. The old man who owned the place before us kept the loft for storage and put his car down below. I guess there's still lots of his junk out there. He promised to pick it up. But he hasn't. Mom's threatening to throw it all out. Haven't looked at it myself."

"We will do that tomorrow. You and I," said Julie.

"I hate climbing ladders. It's scary and hard work. Makes me sweat."

"It will get easier," said Julie.

For a moment I had this mad feeling that like Alice I had fallen down a hole into some wonderland and that the character speaking to me was the Queen of Hearts who any moment would shout "off with his head." I could feel Julie's strength, her determination. It was confusing, dismaying even. "I doubt that climbing ladders will get easier," I said.

"Oh, yes. As you lose weight, it will get easier. You'll see," she said. And she smiled at me.

"I am not going to lose weight," I yelled. "I will be as fat as I want."

"But you will not wish to be so very fat. Each day you will wish it less. I will help you. And you will help me find the horse."

If there's anything that staggers me, it's to have some do-gooder decide you need help. I was seething with hatred. And the hatred made my teeth chatter. I could barely speak. It took control to say in even, nasty tones, "There is no horse anywhere near this place."

"Oh, but there is. Diablo Grande is here. And I must find him. We will find him together. You'll see."

Mom came to the door and said, "Dinner is ready. Come children."

That was the first normal, useful statement I'd heard for some very long minutes. But I was so staggered by this kid and her strange ways that I

sat there, not moving, "Jumping Jehoshaphat!" I
whispered. Now she had me doing it.

Julie didn't turn her head. She was already in the
dining room. So were Mom and Dad. "I . . . I
don't feel hungry," I stammered. Anger can make
it hard to get words out. "I'm going upstairs. Excuse me, please."

And as I was climbing the stairs, I heard Julie's
whispery voice. "Jumping Jehoshaphat, but dinner
looks good," she said.

Oh, oh . . . the kid was imitating me already
and her words made me cringe. I sat down on my
bed, a little dazed. Because I really truly wasn't
hungry. I was too baffled, confused and scared.
Where had Julie come from?

2 Diablo Grande

Next morning when I woke up I felt awful. For a few moments I considered spending the day in bed. Only the longer I lay there the drearier such a prospect seemed. Mainly because I was absolutely starving to death. What could have come over me that I had refused to eat dinner last night? I was sick all right. Sick in the head.

I clambered out and pulled on my stout-size blue jeans and extra large sweat shirt. The energy I was expending made me feel faint. I only hoped I could make it to the breakfast table without passing out on the stairs. I pulled open the door and Jumping Jehoshaphat! There was Julie, like a faithful watchdog. She was sitting on the stairs, watching the door and waiting. I had this awful urge to give her a king-sized kick and send her whomping down the stairs. But I didn't. Every now and then civilization rears its head and smacks down instinct. She kind of cocked her head, like a bird, and those yellow eyes, gollee, they about pinned me to the wall. "Hungry?"

"Of course, I'm hungry," I growled. "Pardon me while I go downstairs to breakfast." I stepped over her. "Coming?"

I didn't even look to see if she was. But I needn't have worried. She was coming all right. "You have very different food," she said.

"There's nothing very different about the stuff Mom dishes up," I said. "Just plain old American cooking."

"I suppose that's it," said Julie. "Oh, I do love to experiment," she added quickly. "It is different, though."

Before I could ask her how it was different, Mom was saying "Good morning" and asking us how did we sleep and what we'd like to have for breakfast. Stuff like that.

"You choose, Barney," said Julie.

I ran my hand through my hair, stalling for time. Because I had this peculiar thought, loud and clear. Julie didn't know what to ask for. Seemed odd to me. In fact things were getting odder by the minute. But I didn't let it slow down my appetite. "I'll have bacon and eggs and toast, Mom. Any pancakes?"

"Good heavens, Barney, what are you getting ready for, a weight-lifting contest? No, I don't have pancakes. Bacon and eggs should be adequate. Don't you think so, Julie?"

"Yes, teews ydal," said Julie.

That stopped Mom short. She looked at Julie, puzzled. "What did you say?" she asked.

Whatever it was it wasn't English. Even I knew that. Julie was flustered. "I'm sorry . . . I wasn't thinking. I only said, 'Sweet lady.' "

Holy cow! Sweet lady. And to my mother at that. Mom was stunned. "Sweet lady?" she said. "That was 'sweet lady'? It didn't sound like . . ." She stopped. "Don't call me that, Julie. In this country we no longer use such terms. I really doubt that we ever did. Call me Mrs. Sutton. Or Emily. Either will do."

"Thank you very much . . ." Julie hesitated. "Mrs. Sutton," she said at last.

This gal was a queer one all right. But I didn't let that thought slow down my action. I poured the cream over the dry cereal and ladled on the sugar. A guy needs something to hold him while he waits for his bacon and eggs. And they were worth waiting for. Mom is a wonderful cook. Like eggs, now. She adds cream and fluffs them up and sprinkles in onion flakes and parsley. The bacon is always crisp and salty. I like it that way. Orange juice is always just orange juice. But Mom never lets me escape drinking it. It's got something to do with vitamins.

You'd think she'd be glad if I'd skip anything in the food line. But Mom's funny that way. I have to skip what she wants me to, not the things I don't like.

Julie didn't fall on her food with much enthusiasm. She had no trouble getting the egg into her mouth, but she kept chasing the bacon around the plate with her fork. No matter how often she stabbed it, the stuff escaped. In fact it was crumbling in a small heap of little pieces. "Why don't you pick it up in your fingers?" asked Mom.

"Thank you," said Julie. Only she didn't. I reached for a second piece of toast and some of Mom's homemade raspberry jam, which is about the most perfect jam I've ever tasted. I could see that Julie was watching me, very carefully. It was eerie, like I was performing a new, strange act. As soon as I had the toast buttered and spread with jam, Julie reached for a piece and followed my actions to a T.

"Good . . . ah, it tastes very good," said Julie, chewing very gingerly, like you do when you're not sure you're going to like something. "What do you call it?"

Mom took that right in stride and told her it was raspberry jam. Julie still looked puzzled.

"The bread was toasted. Do you remember doing that in your home?" Mom was trying to piece together something useful about Julie's background. The pieces she was getting didn't make too much sense either to her or me. Not then.

"Ah, I like toasted and raspberry jam. I like them very much."

And Julie smiled. There was something so compelling about her smile that both Mom and I smiled too. You couldn't help yourself. Without thinking I reached for another piece of toast. Four pieces was about my usual breakfast quota and Mom always had plenty, piping hot, just asking to be eaten. Only Julie's hand was suddenly on top of mine, light as a feather. Yet when I tried to lift a piece of toast, I felt as if my hand were permanently glued to the plate, and the plate was anchored in the table. I tugged. In fact I tugged the legs of the table off the floor. But I couldn't get the toast in the air. Julie and I sat there, having a staring match. She kept right on smiling and staring at me. I sat there scowling and glaring at her. But I lost.

"I think we have had enough, don't you, Barney?" said Julie. "Thank you so much, Mrs. Sutton. May I help you?"

She jumped to her feet and carried off the food so swiftly that I was left with my hand hanging over the table, expectant like. "Hey, just a cotton-picking moment," I yelled. No girl was going to run my life for me. No sirreee.

But Mom had scraped the toast into the disposal

and was telling Julie that she was to forget about helping today. Tomorrow would be plenty soon enough. Before I knew what had happened, Julie was asking Mom if Barney could show her around. And Mom said, "Of course."

How about that? Not only did this kid have the colossal nerve to grab the food right out from under me, but she had engineered my serving as guide. Before I could protest, Mom was shoving us toward the outdoors, and, being as big as she is, Mom is hard to resist. Besides, she gave me one of her *you do this or else* looks so I knew that protest would only get me in trouble.

Presto we were on the back porch, leaving. I didn't say a word. The words I wanted to say would only have landed me in more trouble. Julie didn't say a word. I don't know what her reasons were. We were about halfway down the drive when Mom came out and yoo-hooed at us. "Barney, take Julie down to the lake. I'm sure she'd enjoy a boat ride. Have fun."

"Yes, Ma'am," I grumbled, and started off at a run. I was hoping I might lose Julie. But that was a stupid idea. The only thing I lost was my breath. You tire awfully quick when you're fat. I slowed down to a walk and Julie bounced along beside me.

"What's a lake?" she asked.

"A body of water," I answered. If she wanted to play stupid questions, I'd give her stupid answers.

"A body . . ." I could almost hear her think. "A body with legs, and arms and a head?" she asked.

"NO, stupid!" I shouted that. But, how did you explain a lake? It was so simple. But arms and legs? "A lake is on the ground, in hollow places sometimes. Some lakes are fed by springs and run-off. This one is. People swim in it."

"Like your bathtub."

"Not like our bathtub. It's a thousand times the size of a bathtub," I said. "Holy cow, how could a kid who claimed to learn English in three days be so completely stupid?"

"A thousand-times bathtub. How nice," said Julie.

Inside I groaned. If I hadn't been so exasperated at having missed part of my breakfast and then being ordered to serve as guide, I might have turned my brain on. But I didn't. As we rounded a bend in the road, I pointed ahead. "There it is. There's the lake."

Julie's yellow eyes got more intense in color. She ran ahead and stuck her finger into the water and then her whole hand. Why the next thing I knew she had her shoes and stockings off and was wading in it like some three-year-old. And her face had this excitement, this happiness mirrored there. Hey, what was going on?

"I like this lake," said Julie. "We call them aqua dingles. Though I have never seen one so large."

She shaded her eyes and looked toward the opposite shore. "Come on. Let's go out on it," I said, walking toward our boat that was pulled up on the shore. Our property ran down to the water, so we could leave our boat tied up like this. That boat was about the only nice thing that had happened since our move to the country. Dad even let me operate the motor all by myself, which is the next best thing to driving a car.

"Wait . . . Wait, Barney." I wish she wasn't always telling me to wait. "You can walk on this aqua dingle?"

The idea of walking on the water — big, fat, old me walking on the water — was so ridiculous I burst out laughing. And the more I laughed the more I had to laugh, until tears were running down my cheeks.

Julie stood there, staring. I wiped my eyes on my sleeve and started tugging on the rear of the boat to get it into the water. "Come on, Julie, get on the other side of the boat."

She ran around the prow and took hold of the side. "I said something funny?" she asked.

I nodded. "Yep. People don't walk on the water, Julie. We use boats on the water. I mean, it takes a miracle to walk on water. See?"

"I think I would like to see this miracle," said Julie.

"Me too," I said.

The boat slid with a little splash into the water. I

signaled her to climb over the prow and told her
to take the next to last seat. I had to sit in the rear
to operate the motor. Then I shoved us out with an
oar, plunked myself down, and pulled on the cord.
The engine roared into action. Probably the first
time it had caught on the first try since we'd had it.

You can't talk over the roar of an outboard, so I
held my conversation to pointing out things of interest as I'd seen my dad do: the boat docks on the
other side of the lake, the swimming beach with its
rustic dressing rooms, the sailing cove where the sail
club moored its boats, the camping spots, the dam.
Julie kept nodding and moving her lips, like she was
neatly filing each bit of information in her memory
bank. I sure couldn't figure her out.

The sun began getting awfully hot and I knew
that I was going to get a first-class burn if I didn't
get out from under its rays. When you're as blond
as me, your skin burns fast. Hardly had we reached
shore, staked the boat and started back toward the
house when Julie said, "And now the barn."

"There is nothing in the barn," I protested.

"I think there is something there. I feel these vibrations," said Julie.

"Vibrations?" I asked. That was the second time
she mentioned vibrations. She had to be nuts. I'd
never heard of anybody getting vibrations. Sounded
like some exotic disease.

"Yes, Barney, vibrations. That is why I chose your house. Because of the vibrations. Come. We go now."

She took my hand and started in the direction of the barn. Right then, I had had enough. I planted both feet solidly and that stopped her. "What do you mean, 'chose' us?" I asked.

Julie tossed that short black hair of hers. There was a wild look about her. "But, of course," she said looking back at me. "Of course, Barney, I chose you. It was the only way. Come now."

Her words shook me a bit, but I couldn't give in. "I'm not going any place until I get something to eat. So forget it."

"Wait, Barney." Here we went with that waiting bit again. "Here, try this. You will like it." She pulled something out of a pocket and dropped it in my hand.

I stared at it and knew that she had to be kidding. Because what she had plunked in my hand looked most of all like a gray pebble. I looked at her for a moment and those yellow eyes locked with mine. I opened my mouth to ask her a question and I couldn't help myself, I popped the stone right down the hatch. I stood there waiting for something to happen. And it did all right. It did. Because I began to taste wonderful flavors. Not just one flavor but many flavors that followed one another as a hound follows the fox. First came deep chocolate that faded to maple that was gradually overlaid with the taste of toasted pecans and marshmallow. Next came grape and raspberry and orange and finally a sharp tangy lemon taste that almost made my teeth shrivel up. Shivers went up my back. It was that sour.

Julie stood watching me. "Now the barn," she said.

Talk about a one-track mind. Julie had it. I was all set to argue. Because I was getting sick of being talked out of eating usual foods like Coke and peanuts and potato chips and candy. But a strange message came through from my stomach. I wasn't hungry anymore. In fact, I didn't even want to think of food. So okay. No use being ornery. I might as well go to the barn and get it over with.

Our barn was sure an old place, filled with dust and shadows and quiet. Dad was threatening to tear it down. But Mom liked its looks and argued that it was plenty good enough to shelter our car and lawn mower. She pointed out that it could even hold the boat in winter. Dad left it standing. It took Julie's and my combined efforts to slide the great wooden door open and to lift the huge, wooden extension ladder so that its top rested against the loft floor. Boy it was heavy! No wonder I hadn't tried to explore this place on my own. Before I could even make a move to get my foot on the bottom rung, Julie had danced up to the top. I took it easy as I followed her.

But once up there, I wondered why I had never thought of exploring the spot before. The only light came from the gabled ends through round glass windows so covered with cobwebs and dirt that only a little light filtered through. The loft itself was a mess of junk. Julie was tugging away at this carton, that box. She seemed to know exactly where she wanted to go. You guessed it. She wanted to reach the farthest, darkest, dingiest corner of them all. Well, don't let it be said that Barney Sutton is a slacker. I began heaving this and that out of my way with enthusiasm. It was hard not to stop and investigate the fascinating objects I was uncovering. There was an anvil, a real anvil. I couldn't budge that. And huge iron tongs and a bellows. There were cowboy boots like I'd been yearning to buy, only these were better. They were worn and scuffed. I wondered if my fat legs could squeeze into them. I passed up bridles and a beautiful saddle and something that looked like a giant dart board. Why I even found some darts. I heaved a few at the target. My attention was off Julie for a moment.

"Aha," she said. It was a very happy "aha" if I'd ever heard one.

I moved toward her in a hurry. She seemed to be dusting at something — something fairly large.

I moved a clothes tree that was in the way and then I saw it. Holy cow! it was a merry-go-round horse. About the wildest one I'd ever seen in my life. Its head was thrown back like it was fighting the bit. Its great yellow glass eyes glittered. Even in the dimness I could see them glitter. And everywhere the horse was jet black except for its bared white teeth and its madly decorated saddle.

"Diablo Grande," said Julie.

"That's the horse we've been looking for?" I asked. "But it's wooden."

"Yes, so you might say. But wood stores memories. This horse tells me he has been here a long, long time. And he is eager . . . eager to be free."

"Aw, Julie, let's not get carried away," I said. My voice was loaded with doubt. "A wooden horse cannot be free. It's impossible for it to be communicating with you. Nobody can communicate with a carved piece of wood. That's crazy."

"It is not crazy. It is a fact. You do not know everything. Where I come from all people know these things are true. And Diablo says he will help me hunt."

"Hey!" I had twinges of worry. Julie was serious. "How do you expect that horse to help you hunt?"

"I expect that you and I will ride him and he will take us out into the countryside to hunt. Don't you see? I must find the escape hatch. It is somewhere I think in a place you call Mexico."

Booby hatch sounded like a more likely thing for her to be hunting. Why, the kid not only had amnesia — she was stark raving mad. And then an overwhelming thought hit me. "If you know that you must hunt for an escape hatch, then you must not have amnesia."

Julie giggled. "Of course I don't have amnesia. But no one asked me if I had amnesia. So I didn't volunteer the information. Was that okay, Barney?"

I nodded agreement. Because there were lots of fuzzy ideas muddling up my think box. Julie didn't wait for me to say anything.

"Tomorrow is too soon for us to go. You must lose weight, Barney. Seven or eight pounds might be enough, I think."

"Great. How absolutely great! Now you're going to try and get me to lose weight so I can go gallivanting around the country on a merry-go-round horse. You've got to be kidding."

"You can do it. I know you can do it, Barney. And Diablo is most eager to be outside again. He longs for the sky and fresh air."

Things were really getting ridiculous. Lucky I didn't have to say anything at the moment, because right then I heard Mom yoo-hooing, calling us for lunch. It was the first normal suggestion I'd heard for a while. "Come on, Julie. Let's go. I'm starving."

And I hustled to the ladder, not even waiting to let ladies go first. "You do not understand," said Julie with her whispery voice. "But you will. Of course. Good-bye, Diablo."

She called those last words toward the corner as she was coming down. And then, over my head, I swear it, I heard a whinny. An honest to goodness horse's whinny. I about fell flat in surprise. I looked up at Julie, wondering. Either that kid was a wonderful ventriloquist or she was telling the truth. She sure was right when she said I didn't understand. And the whole thing had me so upset that I couldn't eat much lunch.

3 First Flight

It was funny that Julie didn't want to go back to the barn the next two days. She said something vague about Diablo's being so eager to be off that we must not tantalize him. She sure spoke in a kooky way. But the barn didn't intrigue me that much. I was perfectly willing to settle for reading or a game of Parcheesi. I never could get Julie to understand Monopoly. Oh, she tried and she really seemed to eat up what she called "new experiences," but she couldn't grasp why anyone would want a monopoly.

One of the oddest things that was happening to me was my disappearing need to eat and eat and eat. Julie urged me to eat one of her candies almost every morning and afternoon. They were always different so that it tantalized my taste buds wondering what was coming up this time. Then when mealtime came, I never wanted to eat much food. I wasn't starving, you understand, but the need to stuff myself was gone. For the first time when I checked my weight on the bathroom scale, I had lost. I couldn't believe it. I'd lost four pounds. Why Mom had had me on diets for months on end and I'd never lost that much the whole dreary time. Besides, I usually had gained back every pound in a few days. Four pounds in two days . . . I couldn't believe it.

And here's a strange thing, once you start losing weight you haunt the bathroom scales. I was on and off them so often that I about wore them out. And the trend was continually downward. You know something, Julie could be right. I might actually lose seven or eight pounds by Monday. I might even lose some more.

Then all trivial things were driven from our minds by my grandmother's accident. This was my mom's mother and one of my favorite people. She'd done an awfully crazy thing — stepped on a tomato peel on her back porch, slipped, careened down the steps and broken her hip. I bet if we had all sat and speculated about crazy accidents none of us would have come up with that particular one. Dad keeps saying that real life happenings are much weirder than anything dreamed up by writers. I couldn't argue with that. Look at us having Julie. Who would ever imagine that my sensible, down to earth mom would volunteer to take in a stray like Julie.

Anyway, Mom left like instantly. She called the

social worker who acted very understanding and said that Julie could stay on with us. Dad told Mom not to worry, that he'd see everything ran smoothly. Now there was a laugh. My dad is so absent-minded that he's actually gone off to teach a class without putting on his trousers.

So Monday came around. I tipped the scales nine pounds lighter than the week before. Julie pronounced the loss enough for the practice flight.

"Flight," I yipped. "Who's flying?"

"We are," said Julie as calmly as if she were talking about the grass being green.

"What are we flying on?" I asked.

"Diablo Grande. Don't you understand? We're flying on Diablo." Julie not only sounded impatient. She looked impatient.

"Look, Julie," I said very carefully, "look . . . Diablo is a wooden horse. Maybe he is telling you things. Maybe you're making it up. But let me clue you in. Merry-go-round horses do not fly. They go up and down, up and down and always in the same place. Somebody's been fooling you."

"I think not," said Julie and smiled at me.

What was the point of arguing? If she'd ever had experience with merry-go-round horses she'd understand what I meant. Obviously somebody had been leading her on. I almost felt sorry for her. But not too sorry. After all, Julie did like to use big words and startle me with way-out ideas. I still hadn't figured out how she had known the horse was in our barn. But there had to be some simple reason.

Monday morning Julie and I did the clean-up chores after breakfast. I'm not sure Dad even knew where the dishwasher was, let alone understanding that the table and counters had to be wiped and the food put away. Then there were the beds to make and the papers to throw out. It was almost eleven before we finally headed toward the barn. Julie was somewhat reluctant now. I couldn't figure out why. Not right away. She'd been so eager earlier that her present slow tread and worried look seemed peculiar. Then it dawned. Of course. She realized now that the game was up, that we'd go up to the loft and there would be Diablo, that we'd climb on him and nothing would happen. It's hard to have a hope collapse, no matter how wild a hope it has been.

I suddenly felt sorry for her. "Hey, Julie," I said, a little gruffly, because it's hard to be kind to some people. Especially someone as irritating as Julie. "It's okay, Julie. I don't mind if we don't fly off somewhere. I mean, Diablo is a great horse anyway. Maybe Mom will put him in the house when we tell her about him. She likes way-out things like a merry-go-round horse in the living room."

Julie said nothing. I took a look at her. Why, she hadn't heard a thing I had said. Her face had a vacant look like her mind was off somewhere. She came to with a start. "Oh . . . oh . . . Barney, I'm sorry. What did you say?"

I couldn't say it again, not if my life depended on it. "Nothing," I muttered.

We stepped into the barn. "Ah, you were asking about the flying," said Julie.

"Who me?" I asked, stupid like.

"You are a kind, thoughtful boy, Barney. I like the way you kept quiet and let me try to remember the procedures."

"Sure, sure — that's me. Barney Sutton, Boy Scout." I was clowning a bit.

"You see," said Julie going right on, "Diablo's equipment is so very old."

"Yeah, I noticed. Why his paint looks like it was put on about a hundred years ago," I said. "And the leather in the stirrups is about to give way."

"It is not the stirrups or paint that worries me. It is the transductor."

"No kidding," I said. I was hearing her words loud and clear, but I wasn't understanding them.

"And then there is his name. Diablo means devil you know — in Spanish. I do not understand exactly what that means, devil. We have no devils in my country," said Julie. "But I sense that it is something bad. Diablo might not be trustworthy."

Imagine having a conversation with a girl smack in the middle of the day in plain sensible Iowa about whether a wooden horse was trustworthy. I couldn't say a word. They all jammed up trying to get out of my mouth. The lack of words on my part didn't stop Julie. She kept right on talking. "Of course, since Maharba Nlocnil brought him here, Diablo must be all right. Nlocnil was such a wonderful person. He came to help your country, you know."   **1690329**

"Listen, Julie, you've gotten countries mixed up. Never has there been anyone here by that name, helping or not helping. It's not a name you could forget. Sounds more Russian or Serbian the way the letters go together. Maybe you're mixed up completely." I wasn't saying it too clearly, but Julie was sounding more nuts by the minute.

"Still, a transductor is a transductor. I should be able to operate it," said Julie. How about that? She wasn't listening to me at all.

"Pardon my stupidity," I said, "but what is . . . a trans . . . transductor?"

The way Julie's yellow eyes snapped you'd have thought I had said I didn't know what a zipper was or four wheel drive. I could feel the blood surging up into my face. Yep, I was blushing. I do that when I'm embarrassed. But what the heck! I really didn't know. "Oh," said Julie, "of course. You do not use them yet, do you? A transductor picks up energy from one source and changes that energy into a different and stronger power that it can use."

"Very sensible," I muttered. I didn't have the

foggiest idea of what she was talking about, but I wasn't about to let on. "And that's how we're going to operate Diablo?"

"Of course," said Julie. "It's the only way. Only I do not know what primary energy source we should use. Perhaps the sun — it is steady and more stable than some other types."

"You could say that," I said.

"Yes, I do say," said Julie. "Still, if you think I should try, I might attempt to split an atom."

Hey, at last we'd hit a subject that I understood. At least the words had a familiar sound. "Just a cotton-picking minute!" I really exploded. "You aren't standing there telling me that you can split atoms?"

"It is not easy," said Julie. "But when you reach my level of training we have done all the basic steps in splitting atoms. Still, here in this different land . . . something could go wrong. Should I try, Barney?"

I shook my head back and forth, slowly, sadly. "No, I think you had better forget the atom bit." Holy cow! Imagine trying to explain to Mom that we had blown up the barn trying to split an atom. Thank heavens Julie appeared satisfied with my decision. She simply turned and bounded up the ladder to the loft. I took it more slowly . . . thinking . . . thinking. I didn't come up with anything useful. When I got topside, Julie was over in the corner, tugging at Diablo.

"What do you think you're doing?" I asked. Julie looked like she was going to take the horse on for a wrestling match.

"We must get him downstairs so we will have room to operate. Please, Barney, help me?"

I had to be out of my mind. What she suggested was work. But I helped her. It took both of us, heaving and struggling, to get Diablo over to the ladder. Man, that horse was heavy! I have to admit I rather expected that once we had him in position, Diablo would make use of his transductor and get down to the barn floor under his own power. But no such luck. Julie and I had to do it. We tied a rope around his middle and I looped it over the four by four supporting the roof. That way I had leverage. Julie grabbed hold of Diablo's wildly tossing head and helped to steady him as I lowered away. She had a problem keeping pace with my lowering. Hanging on to a horse's head and managing a ladder's rungs at the same time can be rough.

I had hardly reached the barn floor, when Julie shot by me and back to the loft, hunting for something. Turned out to be a stand, a black square metal piece that sat on the floor. Through it went a pipe about three feet high. On top of this pipe was a gigantic spring. Then came a short piece of pipe.

"We must lift Diablo onto this," said Julie.

I didn't argue. If we must, we must. So we did. His wooden belly fit down onto the spring. I gave him a little push, just experimenting, and he began rocking in a mad gallop . . . up and down, up and down. Made me seasick to watch him. That horse could move. A moment later here came Julie with a tall brass pole. It fit into a hole in Diablo's back and went straight up to the loft floor, fitting snugly under it.

"Next we need our suits," said Julie. And back up the ladder she scampered.

The kid was amazing. She was going to carry this whole crazy thing through to the final moment of truth when she and I would climb on Diablo's back and there we'd be, bouncing up and down in the barn. Oh, well. It wasn't worth an argument. I might as well see it through.

I hardly blinked an eye when Julie handed me the brightest orange jump suit I had ever seen and a tight-fitting white skull cap. But I gave her a piece of my mind when I saw the mask. It was shaped to cover the front half of a person's head. There was a bulge where it covered the ears and greenish glass over the eyes.

"Just a minute, kid," I said, "you aren't serious about me putting that on, are you? I haven't played dress-up since I was a little guy. And it never was my favorite sport."

"But without it — the mask — you would die
. . . the speed . . ." Julie looked at me, her yellow
eyes almost spitting sparks. "You are very foolish
if you do not put it on."

But she didn't argue. Instead she started pulling
on a brilliant pink jump suit right over her clothes.
It was a duplicate of mine. Her comment about
speed and being foolish . . . ? Okay, so who would
know if I humored her and put it on. I was beginning to get this squigidy feeling in my spine that
Julie was really, truly nuts. No point in setting her
off.

The suit was a terrific fit, sort of snugged around
me after I got it on, as if it were molding itself to
me. And the face mask. Now that was crazy. It
clamped on like my own skin. I thought I was
going to smother — I don't like things so close
against my nose. "HELP!" I shouted.

And Julie flipped over, like you do in a hand
stand. "Hey, Julie. What's the matter. Hey,
Julie . . ."

Suddenly Julie's voice was in my ear, a whispery
voice. "Barney, do not shout. The transceiver is
very sensitive. A whisper is best."

"A what? a trans . . . what?" I dropped my
voice to a whisper.

"The head pieces . . . each one has a transceiver
. . . a small transmitter and receiver all in one.
Speak softly, softly. My ear drum is in agony."

"Sorry about that," I whispered. "How was I to know? I thought I was smothering. How come I can breathe, huh?"

"The oxygen adjusts itself to the necessary level automatically. It comes from the energy source. And now we are ready. Shall we go?"

I was ready all right. I felt silly, but I was sure ready. Julie hopped onto Diablo's saddle. Now merry-go-round horses don't seem to have very deep saddles. This one was almost flat, making the end of the saddle and the end of the horse about level. So all I had to do was get my sitting equipment squeezed onto the horse's rump. Wasn't easy. First off, I couldn't get my leg over the back . . . it was a fairish ways off the floor. I almost tipped Julie and Diablo over in my attempts. Next I dragged over a carton, stepped up and right through the top. I had the darn thing around my knees. Okay, no one as heavy as me should expect cardboard to hold him up. I was ready to give up. But Julie's eyes fastened on me and I felt embarrassed. I eyed the stirrup, but it was full of Julie's foot. Then I spotted the trunk. It was an old thing Mom had talked about refinishing sometimes. I dragged it beside Diablo, climbed up and stepped into place. We began gently bouncing, up and down on the spring. Up and down, up and down. I giggled. Me Barney Sutton past twelve and bouncing on a merry-go-round horse.

"Where do you suppose," came Julie's whisper, "the transductor is?"

"The tail?" I asked.

"No, no. There would be no sense in that."

"How about an eye? They've got an unnatural glitter."

"It must be readily available to the rider," said Julie.

"Hear, hear, how about an ear," I shouted.

I had forgotten. Julie jumped so violently that Diablo seemed to leap. "Sorry, Julie, I forgot," I whispered.

"You are right. It is in the ear. So I will adjust the dials and twist it in just right. We are ready . . . Now concentrate."

"I hate to be dull," I said, "but where are we off to?"

"This should be a practice run. Do you not think so?" asked Julie.

"Yeah, I sure think so. Let's not get too ambitious," I whispered.

"You choose."

I couldn't think of a place at that moment. She was offering me a trip to any place in the world and I sat there. "How about your grandmother's house? That is not far," said Julie.

"The heck it isn't. It's almost 500 miles."

"That's just what I said. It isn't far. What do you call the place where she lives?" asked Julie.

"It's a town called Yellow Springs. And it's in Ohio," I answered, exactly as if I thought something might happen.

"Now we must concentrate. You think the name. I will think the name and we will activate the transductor. Ready?"

"As ready as I'm ever going to be."

And then the strangest thing began to happen. The merry-go-round horse began moving, up and down, up and down and around and around in a big circle on the barn floor, exactly like you expect a merry-go-round horse to move. How Diablo was doing it, I couldn't figure out. And I didn't have much time to do any real figuring, because before we'd made the circle twice we were moving faster and faster until I couldn't see the walls of the barn or the open door. I couldn't see anything but a blur of yellow light. I heard myself gasping. Mainly because I was getting scared. Really scared. How long the whirling kept on I'll never know. Maybe I passed out. Maybe we crossed some time barrier. I felt lost in nothingness.

We were goners for sure. Diablo was wildly galloping off into nowhere. And then my legs that had been gripping the horse's belly with all the strength in my muscles, my legs began to sense that Diablo's up and down motion was slowing. I opened my eyes. I could see the walls again. And there was the open barn door. Where we had been I had no

idea. But I knew I never wanted to try that transductor thing again.

"Barney," came Julie's whispery voice, "will you
please check the outside. Are we in the right
place?"

That shook me a bit. I wondered where she
thought we might be. But for once I didn't smart off.
I simply slid off Diablo's back and started toward
the door. I felt strange as I walked, like you do
when you've been horseback riding. The ground
was sort of heaving up and down. I stepped outside
to take a look. And Jumping Jehoshaphat! I wasn't
in Iowa. That wasn't our old farmhouse out there.
It was my grandmother's. Honest to heaven, somehow, someway, Diablo had whipped us to Ohio. I
was so surprised, I just stood there staring.

4 Never Tease a Gossip

I DON'T KNOW how long I stood there like that, staring at the house. It took a while for my brain to accept the message it was getting from my eyes. How had Diablo done it? It was impossible — impossible and scary. Had our whole barn come with us? Now that idea I could check out, and fast. I knew for a fact that Grandma was going to be mighty huffy about a barn in her flower garden. I turned around, but there was no barn. Julie and Diablo were plainly visible, but the barn was gone. Yep, there she sat gently bouncing up and down, up and down, right smack in the middle of my Grandma's choice roses. For a moment I thought Diablo was going to snatch one of the great red blossoms in his mouth. But that was a silly thought. Diablo was wood, wasn't he? Besides, his head was still tossed frantically back in the same wild attitude as always. It dawned on me that his head was turned toward the right ear, toward the ear that held the transductor. Maybe he was trying to figure out how to use it. That gave me an extra shiver in my boots.

"We are in the right spot, Barney?" came Julie's voice in my ear.

"Sure looks like it. Come on. Let's go in. Why Grandma might even have some cookies in the cookie jar. She's a great cook. And I am starving." Which wasn't surprising. It must be way past lunch time.

"Just a moment, please," said Julie.

I couldn't figure what she was doing, twisting the right ear smack out of its socket like that. Then she pried up a little metal object, dropped that in her pocket, screwed the ear back in and swung off the horse.

"What did you do that for?" I asked.

"I do not trust Diablo," whispered Julie. "He has been in your world too long. Think of the trouble we would be in if he took off on his own. So I take care. See, here is the transductor. Without this he must stay where he is."

I stared at the thing in her hand. It was about the size of Mom's watch and had three tiny dials on it. Crazy-looking thing. Julie slipped it back in her pocket. I gave her an absent-minded nod of approval as I led off toward the back porch. I could just see Mom's expression if she walked in on us. And wow! Can't you hear us trying to explain how we'd flown in on a wooden merry-go-round horse? That would be a tough one for Mom to swallow. And how the suits weren't costumes, they were for real space flight or was that a time flight instead? The whole picture made little bubbles of laughter gurgle inside.

So you can see that I wasn't looking next door where Mrs. Puckleheimer lived. Now there was a real character. Not only a character but a born snoop. If anything unusual was going on in Yellow Springs, you could count on Mrs. Puckleheimer being the first to know. We had visited Grandma many a summer and Mrs. Puckleheimer had been awfully busy calling Mom to ask "if Barney had permission to take the watermelon from Mr. Battle's field" (I didn't) or "did Mom know that Barney had been swimming in the stream" (she didn't) or "was Barney supposed to be painting the little Hansen girl with red paint?" (I got a licking for that.) Oh, she was a great friend to the kids — Mrs. Puckleheimer was — like Blue Beard and arsenic. And she knew me.

Except, of course, today I was pretty well covered up in the tight-fitting orange jump suit, white skull cap and fantastic face mask. I suppose if I'd met myself face to face I'd have been a little scared. But not Mrs. Puckleheimer. She came through the hedge like she was one of the charging Light Brigade. "Just a moment there . . . you . . . you creature, you."

She must have been yelling but the words were muffled behind my mask. I caught a glimpse of Julie diving behind a honeysuckle bush. Which was smart on her part. One masked figure could be a kid playing dress-up, but two in such odd outfits might even frighten Mrs. Puckleheimer.

"It's okay," I said. "I know the people here. They won't mind if I go in."

But Mrs. Puckleheimer charged on. She was big enough to give me the feeling of a tank on the attack. And her nose was twitching like a bloodhound's.

"Barney," came Julie's whisper in my ear. "She cannot hear you. You will have to remove the mask."

"Thanks, Julie. I forgot." I tugged at the thing. It was really stuck on. I said ouch and darn and a few other little words to ease the hurt. It was as bad as pulling off adhesive tape. I got the section around my mouth loose and started pulling up on it. But I didn't get it completely off. Not then. Because Mrs. Puckleheimer had caught up with me, and she was shaking me like I was an apple tree and she was after bushels of apples!

Have you ever tried to think or talk when somebody's rattling you back and forth? I couldn't get words together. They bounced against my teeth and sounded like glunk . . . blug . . . glurg. "You stop that," I finally managed to blurt out. At least my mouth was free.

"Oh, so you can talk, can you?" The shaking kept right on. "If you think you can rob this house just because the owner is in the hospital, you are mistaken. I can have the police here in two minutes."

I believed her. But the way she was shaking me around there wouldn't be anything left to turn over to the police — just a heap of disconnected bones, teeth and hair.

"Help, help me!" I could barely get the words out. They weren't loud, but the transceiver was still close enough so it carried to Julie.

And help is what I got. Julie tore off her own mask, jumped out from the bush and came charging toward us, shouting. "You let him alone, you wicked thing, you. Let Barney alone!"

Mrs. Puckleheimer only got a glimpse of Julie as she attacked — a shocking-pink shape with tight-fitting cap and flashing yellow eyes. Julie butted into her exactly like a billy goat on the attack. She caught Mrs. Puckleheimer in the rear and her momentum was so great that the mountain of a woman lost her balance. All three of us went down, me on the bottom, of course.

Mrs. Puckleheimer didn't say anything. She just lay there quiet like. Julie picked herself up first, and finally between us we rolled the fat woman off me. We left her lying there, just quietly. I think it was the very first time I had ever seen Mrs. Puckleheimer's face without a snoop or sneer on it. She looked peaceful. For a moment I had felt scared. Is that the way people looked when they were dead? Then I saw her chest going up and down. I nodded to Julie and we both turned and ran toward the house.

Grandma always left the house open, so we had no problem getting in. Quick as a flash I locked the door behind us and then tore off my face mask. It felt good to be able to breathe ordinary air. We left the masks in the kitchen while we explored the house. It was Grandma's all right. But here's a strange thing . . . the house didn't feel right somehow . . . not with Grandma gone. It had an empty feel, a hollow feel.

"Maybe we ought to go," I said. "No telling when Mrs. Puckleheimer will decide to go into action again."

I happened to glance toward the window on the back porch and oh help! the queen of the snoops was crouched down, peering inside. The kitchen was pretty dim, so I suppose she couldn't see us too well. But well enough. "Is that you, Barney Sutton?"

Her voice was shocked . . . not only shocked but kind of triumphant. "Well, young man, I shall just call your mother and tell her how you and your little friend there knocked me down. Yes, knocked

the breath right out of me. You might have killed me."

I didn't say a word, but I turned away so she couldn't see my face at all. Then using a squeaky tone I said, "Why don't you do that, Ma'am. You just do that right now."

I was egging her on because we had to get her out of the yard. Besides, I could imagine Mom's reaction when Mrs. Puckleheimer complained about my knocking her down. She'd think the old lady had lost her marbles. Still, how I could have knocked down that tank of a woman and landed on the bottom of the heap was a mystery to me. Obviously, it was no mystery to her.

Mrs. Puckleheimer just stood there, not moving. At least there was no sound of boards creaking. And if she moved, those porch boards would shriek. I didn't dare turn to check. The less she saw of my face, the better. Then at last I heard what I was listening for, footsteps moving somewhere. Uh, oh . . . she was trying the handle of the kitchen door. She rattled it. The door stayed shut. At last she gave up. Good thing I'd had the sense to lock it after we were in. Every now and then I do have a smart thought.

"We had better leave now," said Julie. "No cookies, Barney."

My hand was reaching for the lid of the cookie jar. Wouldn't you know, whenever I get a chance to eat, Julie has a good reason why I shouldn't. But I couldn't argue her point. We needed to hustle if we were really to get off. Both of us grabbed our masks and snugged them on. I carefully shut the door behind us and we raced to Diablo. I even managed to get on his back with the first leap.

"Put it in. Put it in," I whispered. I couldn't figure out what Julie was fiddling around for, fingering her pocket, bent over like she was trying to look inside of it. "Barney . . . the transductor. It is gone."

"You've got to be kidding."

"I am not kidding. It is not in my pocket. I feel nothing there."

"The yard," I said. "When we fell, we must have knocked it out."

"But of course. We must hunt for it. Hurry, hurry!"

And Julie was off and flying back toward the spot where she'd made her head-on attack. But when things happen as fast as they'd been happening, you don't pay much attention to the exact location. When Mrs. Puckleheimer grabbed me neither one of us had checked to see whether we'd been ten or fifteen feet from the porch or to the right or left of it. And Grandma's grass was mighty long. Mom ought to get someone to mow it. Why a guy could lose something forever in grass that long. I only hoped we hadn't.

First off we both sort of tramped back and forth, looking this way and that. No luck. We tried going crossways. Still no luck. "Hey," I said, gasping a little. Panic was beginning to set in. "Let's get organized. If we'd crawl on our hands and knees leaving space between us, we could search the grass with our hands. That's the only way we're going to locate the thing. Okay?"

"Very sensible," said Julie. "Why didn't I think of that?"

We dropped down and started slowly feeling our way across the space. We felt every inch in a five-foot strip back of the porch. Then we turned around and started back on a new section which had us facing the hedge. And I could see what was coming next. Mrs. Puckleheimer. Mrs. Puckleheimer under full steam like a battleship was coming toward the hedge. "Hurry, hurry," I said. And crawled faster.

I was feeling with my hands, keeping one eye on the hedge. And then I felt it . . . a hard, round, metal case. I snatched at it. "Got it, Julie. Let's go."

Julie grabbed it from me and ran toward Diablo. I couldn't keep up. When you're fat, it's hard to move that fast. Still I was moving faster than a week ago. I kept my legs chugging up and down like pistons. Julie was on Diablo's back. She had the ear out and was easing the transductor into its hole. I made a leap for the horse's rump and made it. And my heavy landing started us bouncing, up and down . . . then round and round.

Now here's a crazy thing. I looked around and I thought we were back in the barn, our very own barn at home. Yet through the barn door I could still see Mrs. Puckleheimer, fat and puffing, bearing down on us. She really looked like she was about to explode. Her face was purple — she was that angry. And she was yelling something that sounded like — "You . . . you things you. Stop this minute. I want to talk to you. Stop! I say."

"But we do not wish to talk to you," whispered Julie in my ear. I snorted. "We are ready, Barney. Think of home, please."

And I thought of home. I thought the idea *home* as hard as I could. Round and round, faster and faster we whirled. Mrs. Puckleheimer became a fuzzy blob. Her voice said disconnected things. "Not in the roses . . . you are trampling the roses . . . don't you dare come closer." Then her image and voice were both gone as we plunged into that yellow void where speed and brilliant flashing colors made me black out.

Next thing I knew, Julie was saying, "Well, Barney, are you going to sit there all day?"

I opened my eyes. There was the barn door, still open. But no angry old lady was in sight. I got off, tired all the way through. Automatically I peeled off the mask and the cap and the suit, handed them to Julie and headed for the door.

"Just a minute, Barney. We must rub Diablo down and hide him away."

"Oh no." I groaned at the thought of more action. But I helped. Though I said flat out that I couldn't pull Diablo back up to the loft. I suggested maybe there was some place on the main floor to hide the horse. And sure enough, we found a great spot behind a huge old garden umbrella that Mom had once used in the yard. By shoving the trunk in front of that, Diablo couldn't be seen.

Then we hiked into the house. I excused myself and headed for my room. The only thing I could think of was how good my bed would feel. High flying was exhausting. And confusing. Because when I looked at the clock, Jumping Jehoshaphat! We'd hardly been gone an hour. Now that's what I call speed.

5 No Matter How You Spell It, Danger Means Trouble

I MUST HAVE BEEN tireder than I thought, because I don't remember falling to sleep. I was just gone. And the next thing Dad was hallooing from downstairs. Took me a few minutes to get myself oriented. I thought it must be morning. But no, it was only five in the afternoon. Dad was home from the University and trying to find out where Julie and I were hiding. I gave him a grumpy answer and rolled out of bed. In fact I still felt groggy when I got downstairs. Sleeping too much can do that to a guy. I didn't revive until I had had a Diet Cola and a piece of Julie's candy.

"What have you kids been doing today?" asked Dad, digging around in the freezer to find the TV dinners. "I've never known you to nap in the afternoon before, Barney. You sure you're all right?"

"Sure . . . sure. I feel great."

"Good. Because I don't. It's been a fierce day. I

feel hot, mean, cantankerous. So you and Julie get dinner. Okay?"

"We will be pleased to do that, Mr. Sutton," said Julie. She was acting very formal. She moved over to the stove, set the oven dial and started opening the packages. She looked a little sleepy herself.

Dad was going out the door, a newspaper in one hand and a cold bottle of beer in the other when he turned. "Say, Barney, old man Snodhopper stopped me on the way home . . . waved me down in fact. Said something about this fantastic yellow light from our barn. Asked me if we'd had a fire out there. Were you in the barn this afternoon?"

I gulped. "Well, uhhh . . . sure we were, Dad. Not for long, though."

"You know better than to play with matches in that old structure," said Dad. He wasn't asking. He was telling me.

"Aw, Dad. Come on now. I passed that stage a whale of a long time ago. I don't know what Mr. Snodhopper saw. Must have been a reflection," I said.

"I certainly hope so," said Dad, looking kind of sharply at me. "Well, just thought I'd mention it." He disappeared in the direction of his study.

"Holy cow! Julie," I whispered. I didn't want Dad to hear. "Do you suppose we generated so much light that Snodhopper could see it all the way down at his place? He's a mile away."

"I doubt it, Barney. Perhaps he was walking by. There is a sudden tremendous blast of light at take-off. But it doesn't last long." Julie shoved the frozen dinners into the oven. She was getting as good as me at cooking TV dinners.

"Okay. But we'd maybe better case the area next time before takeoff. If there's one thing my Dad isn't, it's stupid. He'd catch on quick that something was going on if he got too many reports like that."

"What a good decision," said Julie. "Next time we will . . . what did you call it?"

"Case the area . . . Uh, oh . . . that's Dad calling. Wonder what he wants now?"

I hustled into the library. Dad was waiting. "I forgot to tell you," said Dad, "that Miss Bolen called."

"About our bowling," I said, trying to be funny.

"I am not in the mood for your teen-age humor," said Dad. Oh, oh . . . I'd forgotten. Dad was feeling grumpy. I shut up fast. "Miss Bolen is the social worker on Julie's case. She's coming tomorrow, so you two had better stay close to home. She said something about wanting to talk to both of you."

I nodded, but I wasn't feeling happy. Here I'd just gotten my flight wings and Dad was making us stay home. Oh well . . . I went out and told Julie the news. She was almost as happy as me . . . which meant we both felt awful. But we had no choice. That night after dinner we had another surprise — a phone call from Mom. And here's a funny thing. She absolutely insisted on talking to me. "Barney," said Mom, "you are really there, aren't you?"

"Why sure, Mom. Why do you ask?" I had to work hard to make it sound natural. Inside I was killing myself laughing. Old Mrs. Puckleheimer hadn't given up easily. I could tell that.

"I don't know," said Mom. "It's been eerie. Grandma's neighbor keeps calling me and telling me over and over how you and this strange child — a wild child she called her, dressed in a pink outfit — how the two of you knocked her down, ransacked Grandma's house and then rode off on a horse.

"Hey, that's really something," I said.

"I really think she's cracked up, Barney. But she was so convincing that I began to worry that you might really . . . Of course it was silly." I kept very quiet. "To top off the whole thing, she said that these children had a horse tethered in the middle of the rose garden. Now Barney, nobody in his right mind would tether a horse in roses. The poor animal would be scratched to death. And yet . . ." she paused. "And yet, there is a strange circle in the garden now. Everything in that circle looks . . . looks almost as if it were burned." I snorted. "It's all very silly," said Mom, embarrassed. "Let me talk to your father, Barney. Do be good and look after Julie."

What a laugh. Julie needed taking care of like a tarantula needs a watchdog. I went back to the kitchen to finish loading the dishwasher. Julie was carefully wiping the counters. As we worked, I had a sudden thought, one that had been bothering me. "Hey, Julie . . . about the suits we wore. How come you knew where they were?"

She looked surprised. "Why I put them there."

"You put them there?" I asked. I couldn't take it in. "Like when? I saw you arrive. You didn't run out to the barn, that's for sure."

"No, no, silly. When I first arrived. I knew . . . I knew from my sensitizer that there was a transductor in the area. And I remembered about the horse and how Nlocnil had brought such a horse here. He never returned, you know. So the horse had to be close by. You do see?"

Yeah, I could see that. It was a little hard to swallow that sensitizer bit, but still, there was no reason not to. Everything else she had mentioned had come out true, even to Diablo's flying. But knowing about the horse was one thing. It still didn't tell me about the suits. And I told her just that. "Of course," she said squeezing the last drop out of the sponge. "Of course. I thought you knew that I had arrived in a suit. The one you wore was my spare. We always travel with two on a trip like mine. So I hid them in a corner of the barn. I was too tired to do more."

"I didn't know that you were found around here?"

"I walked to that highway . . . Interstate 80 is what they called it," said Julie. "It's only a few miles away."

"That I know. But I can't figure out how you ended at our house. That was a real bit of luck, wasn't it?"

"No, no, Barney," said Julie. "That was positive thinking."

"You don't say."

"Oh, I do say," said Julie. "If one has a clear powerful thought and if it is a good thought then other minds will accept it. In my country we train our minds to be very precise, like fine instruments. We used our positive thoughts to travel today. Did you not know?"

I stood there staring at her. The way she was talking was enough to take the curl out of my very curly hair. The girl was a hypnotist. Maybe she'd hypnotized me. There was a thought to chew on. I said goodnight and went off to bed.

The next day was dreary. First off, there was little to do. We did our chores. Even made a stab at doing some of the piled-up mass of washing. But the air was heavy and dank, the clouds hung low and not a breeze stirred. It was tornado breeding

weather. Seemed like we spent the whole day waiting and it went on forever. Miss Bolen arrived late
in the afternoon. She was a surprise. When Dad
said "social worker" I right away called up this picture of a dried-up, wrinkled, crotchety old woman.
Wow! In walked this gal with silky blond hair
twisted up in some fashion at the back of her head.
Her figure was the kind I'd heard boys whistle at.
But what really came across was her personality.
She had an intenseness that made me think of a jack-
hammer. There was nothing sugar and spice about
this gal.

For the first ten minutes we talked idly . . .
about what we had been doing, the weather and
especially today's weather, how disappointing the
Minnesota Twins had been. Stuff like that. Then
suddenly she began to zero in. "Now Julie," she
said, "have you been able to recall some things . . .
anything? In cases of amnesia, it may sometimes
come back in a flood . . . sometimes in a dribble.
Do you remember anything?"

"Oh, yes," said Julie in a happy way. "Lots of
things."

"Do you remember your name?" asked Miss Bolen.

Julie nodded agreeably, but said nothing.

"Good . . . good . . ." Miss Bolen sat there
waiting. So did I. Only I was beginning to have
panicky feelings. Holy cow! If Julie started telling

her everything, it would be good-bye, Julie. I waited some more. "Your name," said Miss Bolen. Her voice had a slight edge to it.

"Eiluj Daetslos," said Julie.

Both of us stared at her. "Eiluj Daetslos," she said again and slowly, like you might say it for a very stupid child.

Miss Bolen's mouth got a puckered-up look like the top of a potato bag. I think she had the feeling that Julie was pulling her leg. "What nationality is that?" she asked. Only she didn't wait for an answer. "Can you spell it?" Her voice held a challenge.

Julie spelled the name, letter by letter, very carefully. EILUJ DAETSLOS. Miss Bolen sat there staring at the letters on her paper. Just to make sure, she spelled it back slowly. After a pause, she said, "If your name is . . . is . . . Eiluj, why do the Suttons call you Julie?"

Now it was Julie's turn to look surprised. "Why because in your language, that is the translation. I thought you'd know. My name translated into English is Julie Solstead."

That information brought a dazed look to Miss Bolen's face. She kept on staring at the letters. I stood at her shoulder staring at them myself. I guess we both caught on about the same time. "Good heavens, child. You are inverting words . . . you are spelling backward."

"No, no," said Julie. "I believe it is you who are

reversing words. We spell ours forward. Oh . . .
I am sorry. I should never have said that. My father
would say it was not polite."

Miss Bolen had the good sense to blush. Because
Julie had suggested the social worker was being
rude. The room was very quiet. Then the question-
ing routine began again. "You know where you
live?" asked the social worker.

"Oh, yes," said Julie.

"Heck, Miss Bolen, she lives here. She isn't stupid," I said. I stood directly behind the woman and
formed the word no very distinctly with my lips.
Julie caught on.

"Yes, I live here," she said, "with the Suttons."

"I did not mean at the moment. I was asking
about your home — where you really live."

"Oh that . . ." said Julie, and let her voice fade
away. Miss Bolen did not pursue it.

"Can you remember what your father does?"
asked the woman.

"Of course. He is a teacher. A teacher of scientific matters at the third level."

"The third level?" Miss Bolen repeated the words
like a puppet.

"She means college," I blurted out. "That's the
way they organize education in her country, different levels, see?" I tried to attract Julie's attention,
but she wouldn't look my way. I had to warn her.

"You remember things very distinctly, don't you,"

said Miss Bolen. "Tell me more."

I had to stop Julie. If that kid kept on telling everything she could remember she'd be off to the booby hatch in no time flat. I had to save her. Do something.

"Pardon me," I said to Miss Bolen. "May I borrow your paper and pencil for a moment?"

Without her pencil, Miss Bolen seemed at a loss. The questions stopped. I wrote out the word danger. Then I rewrote it backward, tore off the sheet, handed the tablet to Miss Bolen. The questions started again.

"What were you going to say, Julie?"

"You asked me what I could remember . . ."

I flashed the paper with the word Regnad at Julie behind Miss Bolen's back. Her face got white. She seemed to be having a very hard time finding words. "I feel very confused," she whispered. She looked it too.

Miss Bolen wasn't the least bit discouraged. She turned on me next. I couldn't figure out why. She asked me what we'd been doing and I mentioned the boat ride and our games and exploring the barn. I stuck to the truth. Then she asked me what I had learned. Now if I'd thought for one teensy moment, I'd have caught on to what she was after. But I was so carried away with our mad adventure of yesterday that I started to tell her what had happened before I could catch myself. I was about

midway in the flood of words about transceivers and transductors and how the latter could transform energy into power when Dad came in with the groceries. "Hi, Dad," I said.

His sane, very normal presence brought me back to the moment with a jolt. Holy cow! What was I doing blabbing everything I knew to Miss Bolen. Too much talk can be dangerous. Miss Bolen didn't seem to mind my silence a bit. She said, "Good afternoon, Dr. Sutton," and went on to say that she'd been having a very interesting chat with us. And

that she had come to a decision. Do you know what
her decision was? To send Julie to a mental hospital.

"Tut, tut, tut," said Dad, clicking his tongue
against his teeth. Dad always says tut, tut, tut like
that when he's upset and needs a bit of time to get
his thoughts in order. "I think you are being hasty,
Miss Bolen. The child has been here two weeks.
She seems a perfectly normal child to me except for
her lack of memory."

"I have just discovered that she is a classic ex-
ample of reversal," said Miss Bolen. Made Julie
sound like she had some dangerous disease. "Obviously you are overstimulating her here."

"Overstimulating her?" Dad was taken aback.
"In what way?"

"The intellectual atmosphere is creating fantasies
in her mind. She can't separate reality and unre-
ality. Why when you arrived, Barney was spouting
all kinds of scientific gobbledygook. I wouldn't be
surprised at all if she isn't having a bad influence on
him. She's . . ." Miss Bolen looked at Julie a moment, searching for the right word. Julie was something to look at, too. She was frightened and a little
frantic. "She's a wild one," said Miss Bolen.

"A wild one?" The words jarred me. I shouted
them back at Miss Bolen, daring her to say that
again.

"Just look at the child," said the woman.

And we did. I got a shock. Because Julie was

tossing her head like Diablo. I wanted to tell them that all Julie wanted was to go home. To be free. But I didn't have the chance. Because Dad was getting excited himself. I think he sensed Julie's fear and he was angry at Miss Bolen for frightening her so. Besides, Dad hates arguing with women and most of all he hates scenes. I've heard him tell Mom that women argue in zigs and zags, changing the subject with a twist of the tongue. He resented Miss Bolen's shifting from Julie's mental condition, to our overstimulating her, to her having a bad influence on me. He didn't know which statement to attack first. So he took the obvious.

"Well, Miss Bolen," Dad was speaking very quietly, but each word came out wrapped in emphasis. "You are right about Julie's influence on Barney. It has had a remarkable effect. She is actually getting the boy to lose weight. I do not know how she is doing it. But Barney has lost five or six pounds since she's been here, haven't you, son?"

"Almost twelve pounds, Dad," I said.

"I told you. I told you," said Miss Bolen, wildly. "For a growing child to lose twelve pounds so fast. She's dangerous. Not only wild, but dangerous."

"Don't exaggerate, Barney," said Dad. I recognized I'd made a mistake and shut up. "As far as our overstimulating the girl intellectually . . . surely, you realize that we do not speak of scientific subjects in this house. I do research, yes, but in the field of language. Pure science is not our forte. The kind of scientific nonsense like Barney was spouting is not generated here."

"Barney wasn't spouting," said Julie, leaping to my defense. "He was telling the true facts he had learned. Miss Bolen had asked Barney to tell her what he had learned and he was doing that. My father is a scientist and I know when facts are correct . . . like transmutation."

"What in the world?" The question popped out of Miss Bolen, surprising even her. She stared at Julie.

"Why you know what that is," said Dad. "The old alchemists were trying to accomplish transmutation when they attempted to change lead into gold. It's an old idea. An unusual one for children this age to be discussing, but still, hardly anything startling."

But Miss Bolen ignored Dad. She was staring at Julie. "Are you trying to tell me that you understand transmutation?"

"Indeed I do," said Julie. "I've helped in the experiments. It works, you know."

"You have turned lead into gold?" asked Miss Bolen. She acted as if Julie had just sprung a second head.

"Oh, no," said Julie. "I never tried."

"See, there," said Dad. "That's a very normal answer, if you ask me."

"Because you see," said Julie, "we usually turn gold into lead."

"And that, Dr. Sutton, is hardly what I would call a normal reply," said Miss Bolen triumphantly.

I burst out with a loud haw-haw. "She's only pulling your leg," I said. "Kidding. Julie's a great kidder, aren't you, Julie?"

I hauled off and gave her a hard kick. She let out a yip. Dad caught a glimpse of what I had done. Well, he was irritated with Miss Bolen which made him doubly irritated at me. "Take the groceries to the kitchen, young man. And don't let me catch you kicking a girl again."

"Regnad . . . regnad . . ." I muttered to Julie as I went by. She shut up.

"I told you, Dr. Sutton, that I feel it is necessary to have this child transferred. Since there is doubt in your mind, I will call Dr. Greenman and get his approval." Miss Bolen moved toward the phone.

I stopped with the groceries in my arm and watched her dial, kind of hypnotized. If they took Julie away she could never find that escape hatch. I heard the little whisper . . . "pleh . . . pleh."

That sounded so much like please, that Miss Bolen turned from her dialing and said, "Yes?" If she'd used her brain she'd have known that Julie was only calling for help.

"Positive thinking," I said, coming to life. "Positive thinking."

And I began thinking positively like mad. I only hoped Julie was too, because I was pretty new at using my brain this way. Miss Bolen stood there, holding the receiver. Dad stood there, red-faced, angry, distraught. We were all standing like statues. And then, and then, Miss Bolen put down the phone. "Perhaps you are right, Dr. Sutton," she said. "We will wait awhile. It might be precipitous to move Julie. I will leave her for the moment." She picked up her purse. "I am not quite sure why I am doing this, except that it suddenly seems the right thing to do."

She left without saying good-bye. "Nasty, nosy woman," said Dad.

I'd been thinking that identical thought myself. "Positive thinking," I said to Julie and we both grinned.

"Go on, children . . . go somewhere and play quietly, will you? Scenes like this upset me." And Dad sank down in a chair with the newspaper.

"Hey, Julie." I was lugging the groceries to the kitchen. "I've got an idea," I said.

"You have?"

"Yep. Let's start dinner."

Julie gave her head one of those wild tosses and grinned at me. Then we both headed for the refrigerator.

6 The Gold Caper

It's AN INTERESTING THING that it's easier to talk to somebody when you're doing something together than just to talk plain. And I had to talk to Julie. No question of it. But I didn't know how to start. My old habit of grabbing for food to stimulate thinking took over. I reached up and grabbed the potato chip bag. I hadn't eaten any of those things for weeks, but suddenly I had a need to munch on something.

A feather-light hand fell on mine and Julie stood there shaking her head. "No, Barney. Remember, you need to lose more weight."

"How much do I need to lose, I ask you? I did all right on Diablo yesterday, didn't I? He didn't break up or anything because of my weight."

"Perhaps yes, perhaps no. I thought we tilted backward a bit. Diablo is not geared to carry two people. You must lose weight, Barney."

We had one of those eye-to-eye staring matches

. . . her yellow ones bearing down on my plain old gray. I dropped mine first, but I didn't let go of the bag. "I am going to have a potato chip. I may have many potato chips," I said defiantly.

Darned if I was going to let her use her old positive thinking on me. She'd better not try. I ate one, then two . . . okay, you know how it goes. I ate half the box before I stopped. It was a dumb thing to do. But listen, you can't let a girl boss you around all the time, not even if she is smart and knows lots of stuff you don't know.

Julie didn't say a word. She turned away, got out the hamburger and began shaping patties. When I'd finished my binge I grabbed a sharp knife out of the drawer and began slicing onions and tomatoes. The way I went at it you'd have thought I was trying to slash right through the cutting board. It helped to work out my feelings of embarrassment that way. How could I have been so stupid? I hadn't proved a thing by standing up to Julie. I was mulling over something that Dad had often said to me, about how when you make a mistake you should have the guts to admit it and then go on from there. There was no question about the mistake part, but did I have the necessary guts? I hemmed and hawed and cleared my throat. Finally I really made it. "I'm sorry, Julie. That was a dumb thing I just did. I shouldn't have eaten all that stuff."

"It's all right, Barney." She went over and washed

her hands at the sink, carefully avoiding looking at me. "You must do what you think is right, of course."

"It wasn't right. Right had nothing to do with it. I was trying to think of a way to tell you something, Julie."

Now she looked at me, wonderingly. "Tell me? What is it that you find so hard to tell me?"

"You've got to stop talking about what you remember. Don't you understand? That woman — that Miss Bolen — she's no friend of yours. She's an enemy."

"Enemy? I do not think I understand that word," said Julie.

"Try reversing it," I said.

"Ymene," she murmured. "No . . . we do not have such a thing. Can you explain, please?"

Julie might know about transductors and transceivers, but I could see that she was sure missing some important information about people. "An enemy, Julie, doesn't like you. He's out to get you." She looked blank. "You know, kill you off, hurt you." I wasn't getting the message across.

"Kill me? Hurt me? Miss Bolen holds thoughts like that toward me? I do not understand. Why?"

"So who needs a reason to hate someone? It can be the length of your hair, the color of your skin, the way you talk. Any dumb old thing. But believe me, Julie, don't tell Miss Bolen anything — nothing

at all. Or presto, you'll be off to a mental hospital."
Just the thought made me shudder. I'd probably
seen too many TV stories about mental hospitals.
"It isn't a spot I want you to land in."

"But, Barney, we are taught to tell the truth. The
truth cannot hurt you. It can hurt nobody. I always
speak the truth," said Julie.

"Okay . . . okay. So speak the truth. Only quit
volunteering the stuff. And if I shake my head like
this, it means no. And regnad . . . that means shut
up for sure. You did fine with that signal today."

"But Barney . . . I don't understand." I could
see she didn't. "I was only trying to tell them about
transmutation. It is a very important idea, Barney.
After all, that is how I come to be here."

"You're kidding . . . that's impossible."

"No, no! It is very possible. You can see me,
can't you? To get back to my own country I must
find the escape hatch. It has the machinery for
transmuting me. I made a miscalculation, a foolish
one on my trip out. I was going to surprise my
parents with my cleverness, but I surprised myself
instead. And my parents do not even know where
to start looking for me. I must get back."

"Yeah . . . I can see that."

This girl was always surprising me. Her world?
Where was it? Another planet . . . another di-
mension . . . another time? I was afraid to ask.

Sometimes it's easier on the brain not to jam too much new stuff in at once. This transmutation bit was plenty for the moment. I had to chew it over and think about it. And I did. All through supper and cleaning up the dishes. "Hey, Julie," I said, when I'd finished loading the dishwasher. "Hey, Julie . . . what do you think . . . could we turn lead into gold?"

"I told you, Barney. I have never tried. Because we reverse the process," said Julie.

"I heard. I heard," I said. "Why wouldja want to do something dumb like that?"

"Because in my country we have so much gold. Gold is very common. But we have almost no lead and we need lead for many things. So we learned how to transmute gold into lead."

That answer sure set me back. I couldn't imagine a place where they had too much gold. "Do you think you could do it, though?" I was thinking out loud . . . "Change lead into gold?"

"I do not know. I have never tried. But it might be interesting to try," said Julie, "if we can get the necessary elements together."

"How about trying right now?" I said. "Gee, there's nothing but reruns on television and a storm's brewing so we'll have to stay in."

Julie looked at me, her head cocked to one side. She was thinking and her eyes got an inward-looking glaze. Then she was back. "Yes . . . we'll try it. Oh, Barney, what fun to try an experiment on our own. Where shall we work?"

"The basement's the safest. It's got a concrete floor so there's nothing much we can do to it. Come on. Let's go."

Outside the sky was rumbling, muttering. What a great night for the kind of experiment we had in mind. Even the weather was cooperating. First off, Julie said she needed something to mix the chemicals in. We hunted through the basement, looking. I knew it had to be something that Mom wouldn't mind our damaging. I finally spotted the old copper boiler. It was deep and oval shaped. Julie pronounced it excellent, so I lugged it over to the workbench. Next we began collecting the chemicals. I began to feel like a magician's helper and the setting really added to the feeling. The basement walls were made out of roundish field stones that had moss growing on them. There were only a couple of lights and they hung down on cords, the bulbs swinging back and forth with any draft, making the shadows sway in and out of corners. All we needed was a fire and black robes and we'd be properly dressed for the action. My thoughts were weird.

Only I didn't have too much time for thinking. Julie had me hustling for stuff like ammonia and alcohol and sulphur. We were getting one heck of a mixture, that's for sure. What a smell! The kind

that tingled in your nostrils, made your chest burn
and your head fuzzy. I wondered if we should open
a window. But Julie didn't seem bothered a bit.
She stood at the workbench, carefully, carefully
measuring stuff into the boiler. "A mistake . . .
even a little one . . . and pouf the formula will be
ruined. I hope we succeed, Barney," said Julie.

"Me too." I was beginning to get waves of shivers
chasing up and down my backbone. Overhead the
thunder was getting more insistent. And every now
and then the basement lighted up with the blue-
white glow of lightning as it flashed by.

"We are almost ready," said Julie. "Except for
one thing."

"Don't tell me we need something more?" I said.
Actually I didn't think I could stand one more smell
added to the stinking mess in the boiler.

"I think," said Julie with a little flicker of a smile,
"I think that we should find some lead."

I stood there staring at her. Then I started to
laugh. Julie's little smile grew to a big grin. And
pretty soon she was laughing too. Talk about super
dumbbells! Imagine setting out to change lead into
gold and not having any lead. And for a while it
looked as if we'd never find the item. I hunted
under the basement stairs and in Mom's fruit cellar
and all around under the workbench. No lead.

"Maybe we'd better ask Dad," I said.

Lucky for us, he came up with an answer. He

said there was an old scale on the first floor of the
barn and that he would bet there were lead weights
with it. Then he said, kind of out of the blue,
"Aren't thinking of trying to turn lead into gold, are
you, son?"

It was tough having Dad so smart. But I didn't
let on. I grinned at him. And nodded, the kind of
nod that could mean either yes or no.

"No fire in the basement, Barney. That's understood?" he said.

"Of course, Dad. We're not stupid."

I grabbed Julie's hand and we scurried for the
barn. Scurried because rain was beginning to fall.
I stumbled around in the back corner of the barn,
feeling my way. Because the only light we had was
the reflection from lightning. And then I found the
scales. I gave a yip to Julie to clue her in on our
luck. Only she wasn't paying any attention to me.
She was over with Diablo and darned if she wasn't
screwing out the horse's ear.

"Hey, Julie," I said grabbing hold of a ten-pound
weight in one hand and two five-pound ones in the
other. "Let's go." She kept on fiddling with Diablo's
ear. "Hey, Julie, what are you doing?"

"We need energy for the experiment. It takes
tremendous energy to transmute any object. I think
this will do it. I still do not feel quite secure about
splitting atoms, so I prefer the familiar."

Boy, I agreed with her. How I agreed. Splitting atoms didn't seem like something two kids should be doing to amuse themselves on a summer evening. I was glad I didn't have to argue her out of atom-splitting. I signaled her to run. Rain was coming down in buckets. Julie was lots faster than me, loaded down as I was with the weights. We were hardly through the door, when Dad called from the study that we should be sure and wipe our feet well and for heaven's sake to be quiet.

We hurried downstairs. Julie told me to start stirring the stuff in the vat. Holy cow! the odor was enough to knock over a charging bull. I was beginning to get tremors in my stomach, little surges of nausea. I couldn't give up now and miss the show. I held my nose and stirred. Julie eased the lead weights into the bottom of the boiler. "You may stop now, Barney," she said.

And a good thing too. Because I hadn't figured out how I could stir the gunk with the weights taking up space like that. It was suddenly a lot dimmer in the basement. Julie had turned off the bulb over our head and was screwing it out. She had been fiddling around with the dials on the transductor and now she was screwing the thing into the empty socket. My heart began pounding.

"Are you ready, Barney?" she asked.

The smell felt like it was oozing through my skin

— it was going right through me. And my brain recoiled from thinking . . . like something awful was going to happen.

"Ready . . ." The word came out in a squeaky blast.

Julie jerked at the light cord. Jumping Jehoshaphat! The basement exploded. There was a tremendous flash of yellow light which turned bluewhite around the edges. It was so bright it left an image on my pupil like a flashbulb does. And the blast of sound was so tremendous that I thought the walls were giving way. I could hear running steps above us. Dad was shouting, "Barney, Julie . . ."

He had good reason to shout. The transductor was operating all right, all right. It was converting the lightning's energy force through our electrical system into the vat and down into the ground. The liquid began bubbling over the top. The bluish light seared our eyeballs. Julie pulled on the cord. And we were in pitch blackness. The other light had gone out as well.

"Are you all right down there? Are you all right?" shouted Dad, stumbling down the stairs. "What's that smell? Where are you kids?"

I reached out in the dark and found Julie's hand. Then we picked our way toward Dad's voice. It was like blindman's buff. We only found each other because Julie's elbow caught Dad on the hip. He

grabbed hold of us and steered us for the stairs so fast that I skinned my ankle on the bottom step. He was mighty eager to get out of there.

And he didn't slow down when he reached the kitchen either. Now there are certain difficulties in hurrying when a room is dark. And it was very dark in that kitchen. I bet I hit every corner and pointy object available. In fact, it felt like some of them were deliberately reaching out to stab me. Dad didn't stop hurrying until we reached the back porch.

"You wait here. That explosion may have generated a fire. I'll check. Then I'll try to get the lights back on," said Dad.

He came back shaking his head. "Can't get the current back on," said Dad. "You've really done it this time, Barney. And as for that smell . . ."

Julie quietly interrupted. "Could it be perhaps something more than our lights, Mr. Sutton?" she asked.

"Could be, could be. Though I doubt it. I felt that explosion and saw it. I'll call the company," said Dad.

He came back sounding a bit embarrassed and said that the main generator at the plant was burned out. He muttered something about being sorry that he had thought for one minute we two kids had been responsible. I was glad it was dark. I knew I must be looking guilty because I was feeling guilty.

When that Julie girl uses power she really uses power. But burning out a generator? Wow!

Dad used his flashlight to hunt up some candles that Mom kept handy for emergencies like this. I like to use them — they give out such a soft little glow. It's not a lot of light, you know, but it's mysterious. Dad told us to get right to bed . . . it was late. He intended to make another house check just to be sure that the lightning hadn't started a fire. I offered to help . . . saying Julie and I could check the basement. But Dad said no that he wanted to do it himself.

I knew enough not to argue with Dad once he's made a decision. Julie and I did as we'd been told. We trudged upstairs. And as we went up, I could hear Dad open the basement door to start down. Drat! We didn't get a chance to see how the experiment had turned out. I sure hoped Dad wouldn't monkey with the stuff. And the idea bothered me so that I hunted up my hidden Ritz crackers and peanut butter and ate myself to sleep.

7 All That Glitters Is Not Gold

NEXT MORNING I felt awful. Going to sleep on a full stomach always makes me feel droopy next day. And this time was no exception. I staggered like a sleepwalker into the bathroom, brushed my teeth, splashed water on my face. And when I came to enough, I saw the bathroom scale. I hated to get on it. I'd really made a pig of myself last night, like I used to do before Julie came. The scales gave me the bad news swiftly, directly. I'd gained back two pounds. Made me feel like a stupid dope. I really did want to lose weight, but I hated to have people nagging me about it. I was in a black mood when I stomped downstairs for breakfast.

Dad and Julie were about halfway through theirs. And right away I caught on that Dad's mood was almost as black as mine. With good reason. The electricity was still off. That meant no coffee, no toast, no eggs. Everything in the kitchen operated on electricity. Dad was grimly wading through some

Wheaties and milk like he thought it was a newly developed poison. He's always hated cold cereal.

"Young man," said Dad, "I hope you realize what an abominable mess you concocted in our basement. The odor has permeated the whole house."

"Yes, sir," I said. I had caught on fast that the house was stinking something awful. And I didn't need a crystal ball to tell me what was doing it.

"Before you eat breakfast you are to empty that odorous mess out in the woods. Do not dump it down the drain. I am afraid of what it might do to our old plumbing. And I do mean right now," said Dad.

He thought he was punishing me. I let him hold to that thought. Because at the moment I couldn't have cared less about eating. And more importantly, I was dying to see the lead weights. Julie jumped up and offered to help, which was lucky. I wasn't too sure I could handle the copper boiler with both its liquid and weights all by myself.

Man! When I opened the basement door I almost went flat, the smell was that powerful. I held my nose and hurried down. I wanted out of there fast. Julie was right behind me. It was dim down there. The only light we had came through two small windows set deep in light wells. I tried to see to the bottom of the boiler where the weights must be. The fumes started my eyes to watering, and I had the kind of vision you get looking through a rain-splashed windshield. The liquid was reddish green. That's all I could see. I started to reach down and lift out a weight. Julie's hand slapped mine, hard.

"Say, watch it! What didja want to do that for? Huh?"

"I think you are the one that had better watch it," said Julie. "Because I do not know what the energy did to the chemicals. I think you might have your hand drop off if you reach into it."

"You're kidding?" Only I knew she wasn't.

I had this picture of lifting my hand from the gunk and finding only a stump at the end of the arm. For a minute I didn't know whether to shiver or laugh. It was a weird thought. Julie was trying to lift one of the weights using two sticks as tongs. It didn't work. The wood dissolved. We were both coughing a bit now. We had to get out of there. But I was scared to lift the boiler off the workbench. "What if the bottom fell out?"

"Don't just stand there, Barney," said Julie. "Take the handle. We will have to carry the boiler out between us, chemicals and all."

"I don't think we can do it," I said. "The weights alone add up to twenty pounds. That's a lot of weight plus that of the liquid and boiler."

"We shall have to try," said Julie. "Heavy or not."

I couldn't argue with that. Mainly because I re-

membered how Dad had looked when he gave me
the order to dump the stuff. He meant business. So
with Julie gripping one handle and me in charge of
the other, we got the boiler off the workbench. Julie
and I almost went down at the moment we got it
moved off, because the sudden weight on our arms
was terrific. I thought they were coming out at the
sockets. Now the boiler was down, what next? We
decided we'd have to drag it to the steps and then
lift it up, one step at a time. You should have heard
the racket as the copper scraped across the concrete.
Any minute I expected Dad to appear and tell us
to be quiet. Only he didn't.

Slowly, slowly, we inched up the stairs and finally
to the top. But once in the kitchen, we had a problem. Mom had brand-new tile on the floor. She'd
have our scalps if we dared drag that boiler across
the tile. I could imagine what it would do to the
stuff. Julie suggested that we needed something
with wheels. The idea was okay. I stood there
thinking. Then it hit. My old wagon. It even had
rubber tires. That would be great.

"Just a minute," I yelled and tore out the door,
excited that I had actually had a good idea. It took
some real looking in the barn to find the thing. I
hadn't used it for years, so when we'd moved Mom
had stuck it away and gradually loaded it down
with all kinds of junk like tools and old toys and

odd cartons. After locating the wagon, I had to un-load it. I tossed things every which way, just hoping that Dad wouldn't notice.

Then as I was going out the barn door, I had an-other thought. We needed some kind of board to act as a ramp over the stairs. If we tried bumping the wagon down the steps we might bump the liquid all over the steps. Craters might be okay on the moon's surface but Dad would take a dim view of their showing up on the porch steps.

I finally found two boards about five feet long and four inches across. They would have to do. I'd use them like tracks.

It took me a few minutes to get them in place. Then I pulled the wagon up over them. It worked. It really worked. Julie was holding the door open for me. She couldn't miss my rattlely, bangsy ap-proach. And it was a struggle, but we finally man-aged to tug, heave, jerk the boiler onto the wagon bed. It fit snugly. But we'd made it. I was scared that Dad might come in and ask why we hadn't taken the weights out of the boiler. I didn't want to see his face when I gave him the answer. We got out of there, but fast.

On the back stoop, Julie lifted the left front wheel onto the one board and I did the same with the right wheel. She held on at the back and I was at the front guiding and holding the thing. It took all the strength we had. Gravity has more pull than I counted on. The wagon got loose from Julie. It was dragging me down. I held on. I couldn't make it. It started tipping toward me. I jumped like crazy. The wagon lurched, jounced, skewed onto the gravel drive on two wheels — the two on the right side. Naturally it tipped. I stood there horrified, expecting calamity . . . a crater, an explosion? Julie raced by. The whole mess must be going to explode. But I couldn't move. I stood there paralyzed watching the gunk oozing into a reddish-green puddle. The stones were pitting — little holes appeared on their surface. And sprawled in the center of it all were the three weights, black as coal.

A sprinkle of water caught me in the back. I came to with a start. Julie was back, back with the hose, and she was spraying gallons of water into the puddle and the boiler. "Get a pail, get more water!" shouted Julie.

She sounded excited. Julie who was always so calm and contained was as excited as me.

That idea put rockets in my feet. I raced to the basement, found two buckets and tore up to the sink to fill them. I slopped my way outside with one pail, tossed the water into the widening puddle and ran back for the second pail that was filling. In and out, in and out I ran. Being a one-man bucket brigade is exhausting. I began making the trips a little slower and slower still. And help! About the twentieth one Dad came into the kitchen.

"What in heaven's name is going on out here! Why the dashing in and out, young man?" asked Dad. "Don't you ever close a door quietly?"

"Uh . . . uh . . . Excuse me. The pail is full."

I grabbed it, shoved the empty in its place and staggered outside. Dad followed me as far as the door. I passed him standing there when I came back for the next pail. I knew what was coming.

"I told you to dump that stuff in the woods," said Dad.

"Yeah, we were going to, Dad. But I lost control on the steps. It dumped itself right there. And we're trying to thin it out with water," I said.

"H'mm, that sounds reasonable. I'm glad to see you behaving so sensibly. I'm on my way now, Barney. I have a master's exam to attend this morning. You'd better get this floor wiped after breakfast. It's going to need it." ·

He walked down the steps and stopped to look at our puddle. "Oh, Barney. Put those weights back in the garage when you've finished. You certainly changed them all right. I'm not at all sure they are improved." He climbed into the car and was gone.

About then, Julie called off the water action. I turned the boiler right side up, washed it out with the hose, and hauled it back to the basement. When I came back Julie was spraying the weights. We finally got our courage up and lifted them up. I turned the five-pounder this way and that, but any

way I looked at it, it looked worse than yesterday
. . . a little black, somewhat crusted. Man it was
disappointing! I dropped mine and turned toward
the porch. Suddenly, I was hungry. And the work
ahead looked so dull.

Julie didn't come with me. I thought she was
taking the weights to the barn as Dad had told us
to do. At the moment I was too discouraged to do
anything more. I poured some Cheerios into a bowl
and dumped on skimmed milk. Even used the Sac-
charin Mom had hopefully kept around for years,
and which I had carefully avoided for the same
time. If I was going to lose weight, doggone it, I'd
better use my brain instead of my stomach as a
guide when eatingtime came around.

I was about midway through the bowlful when
Julie came dashing in. I thought that maybe the
chemicals were performing or the barn was dis-
solving from contact with the weights. Nothing
would have surprised me. Only I was wrong. Holy
cow! Julie was so excited that she could hardly
talk. When she finally did get something out, she
used my kind of words. "Jumping Jehoshaphat,
Barney! We've done it. I think we've done it."

I looked at the weight she was waving at me. It
was still black and crusty. "I think smelling that
awful stink so long has made jelly of your brain,
girl."

I wasn't going to let her lead me on to hope. I

might not know much, but I was pretty confident
that gold was not black in color.

"No, really, Barney. Look. Look here."

I didn't.

"I took that stiff paper that's rough on one side.
What do you call it?"

"Sand paper," I said, deliberately pouring more
Cheerios into the bowl.

"That's it. Sand paper. And I scrubbed and
rubbed. It took off the black crust in one spot.
Please, Barney. Won't you look?"

I looked. My heart began racing. My throat
tightened. Because what she was holding out toward me looked like the same dingy black weight.
Except for one small glittering spot. It was really
yellow. She could be right. I grabbed the weight,
held it in my hand, scratching at the spot. It must
be gold . . . or was it?

"How can we tell?" I asked. "For sure, I mean.
There is something called fools' gold. I've heard of
that. It looks like the real stuff, but isn't."

"All metals have their own chemical formula,"
said Julie. "We could have it tested."

"I know . . . I know . . ." My words got jum-
bled trying to get out. I felt jittery inside. "I bet
the jeweler in town. He'd tell us. I know he'd tell
us. Let's go ask him . . . huh?"

"Is he friend or enemy?" asked Julie.

That question bowled me over. Julie was a fast

learner all right. I'd only explained the idea of enemies to her yesterday. But I didn't have to consider
my answer for long. "Heck," I said, "Bill Williams
is a friend of my dad's. Mine too. Takes our Scout
troop on hikes. Helps us in our metal work. We
don't need to worry about him."

"I hope you are right," said Julie. "I understand
that gold is valued here. Things that are valued
may sometimes cause trouble."

First we had to do a lot of hard sanding until we
had the whole weight shiny and gold. Then we
faced the problem of getting into town. We solved
that by hitchhiking. I'd never done it before. A
neighbor gave us a lift to the village and then
wouldn't you know, the highway patrol picked us
up. That officer almost wore our ear off lecturing
us about hitchhiking. Man! I was embarrassed at
the way he went on and on. Made me feel stupid.
I was relieved to be dropped at the store. And then
I found myself embarrassed all over again. Mr. Williams is a great guy, but even so, how do you ask
even a great guy if the weight you've got is gold?
I mean, without seeming crazy. It was Julie who
finally asked if he would test this thing . . . this
thing we had found . . . (uh, oh, was Julie telling
a lie?) "Could this thing be gold?" she asked.

Bill said straight out that he doubted it, but he'd
see. And he asked how my dad was and we stood
there waiting. He caught on that we expected him

to do it right that minute. Now Saturday morning is a time that most stores are hopping. Mr. Williams' sure was. He wasn't at all happy to have two kids asking him to examine a hunk of metal. But I'll hand this to him. After he got over his surprise, he went and did it. Sure took him a long time. When he came out he looked — I don't know — kind of hot and upset . . . maybe baffled describes it better.

"Where did you find this, Julie?" he asked.

I jumped in and answered. This was no time for Julie to launch out on the truth, and I was pretty sure she wouldn't keep lying for long. She wasn't used to it. "In the barn," I said. "We found it in the barn." Which, of course, was the truth, but only part of it.

"H'mmmm," said Mr. Williams. "This is very peculiar, puzzling. It looks like gold, but it isn't gold."

"See, Julie, I told you," I said. "Fools' gold. That's what we've come up with."

"You're wrong there, Barney," said Mr. Williams. "It's not fools' gold either. I haven't the equipment nor time to pinpoint what it really is. But it is something unusual. I'm convinced of it. So how about letting me keep it for a while. I've got friends at the University who will be glad to run the tests on it. I don't mind telling you, my curiosity is aroused."

What a spot! I had this uneasy feeling that we ought to just take the weight, go home and forget the whole dizzy experiment. But Mr. Williams was an okay guy, so what difference would it make if we let him fiddle around awhile with the stuff.

"What do you think, Julie? Should we leave it?"

Julie's yellow eyes looked doubtful. "Perhaps. I do not know, Barney. You know such things better. Still, an experiment is nothing if you do not find out what you have found out."

Mr. Williams was busy writing out a receipt to give me. It hadn't crossed his mind that we might not let him keep the thing. He caught Julie's use of "experiment."

"Ah . . . experimenting, Barney? Sounds very scientific. I didn't know you had an interest in science." He handed me the slip, dropping our weight into a paper sack.

"Aw, Mr. Williams," I said embarrassed like, "we were just fooling around."

That started Julie talking. "Fooling around, you say? I do not think that changing lead into gold is fooling around. I thought you were serious. I do not like being made fun of when I am serious," she said.

"Regnad, regnad, you dope," I said.

"Change lead into gold?" said Mr. Williams. Then he laughed. "Always kidding, aren't you, Barney. Who but you would think of trying something like that? Now I suppose you're going to tell me that this thing here was once lead."

"Yes sir," said Julie. "A lead weight . . . Jumping Jehoshaphat!" she gasped. If looks could kill, she would have been a goner. But my warning finally penetrated. Her voice dribbled away.

"A lead weight?" Mr. Williams, his bald head perspiring, stopped to consider that thought. "You know," he said in a surprised tone, "it does look like a weight at that. But I can tell you children one thing. It is not lead now. It could never have been lead."

He looked at me, which was a calamity. Because I was trying to pretend I was listening to him and to form the word regnad with my lips at the same time. It all came together to make a crazy look on my face.

Mr. Williams gave a little start. "Oh, I get it, Barney. Kidding me again, eh? I'll give you kids a ring when I solve the mystery. And watch that kidding, Barney. It could land you in trouble."

He'd said a mouthful there. Only it wasn't kidding getting us into trouble. It was Julie's habit of telling the truth and my greediness. Because, let's face it, when I thought of all the things we could buy if the weights were really gold, I'd got carried away. If I'd known the trouble the weight was going to cause us, I'd have grabbed it and run for my life.

8 A Race for a Wish

I GOT my first whiff of trouble when Dad called me into his study that night after a telephone call and really laid me low. The minute I heard his voice, I knew he was upset. But I didn't tumble about what. I expected Mr. Williams had called. But what do you know — it was the highway patrolman. He asked if Dad knew that his son and his ward were hitchhiking on a busy highway . . . had we told him? Which of course, he didn't and we hadn't. No point going into the lecture, but my ears felt as if they'd been pinned back by words. They even felt hot to the touch. That's how mad my dad was. In a nutshell, he let me know that he did not want me hitchhiking: now, tomorrow or in the dim future. I got the message.

Then he said something awfully queer, sort of chilled me. "You never used to do wild things like this, Barney. Perhaps Miss Bolen is right . . . Julie

is a bad influence . . . like a wild mare introduced
into a barnyard."

How about that? Julie a wild mare and me what?
A hog? I didn't like the picture. Not the least bit.
Julie didn't seem the least bit wild to me. In fact,
she'd been acting quieter and paler for days. Funny
Dad never noticed. But Julie, wild? Different . . .
yes. But not wild. I went to bed feeling troubled
. . . hardly said more than goodnight to Julie. I
was beginning to feel worried.

Next morning was our usual Sunday morning.
We ate late and read the funny papers. By then it
was time to get dressed for church. I almost enjoy
going to church in the village. It's friendly, com-
fortable — warm is the best word to describe it.
After that we headed for Amana. If you like food,
it's the right place for you. Almost makes your
eyes bug out to see the dishes and platters all heaped
up with good things to eat: pickled ham, crusty
chicken, homemade sausage, sauerkraut, and wonderful salad. If you empty a bowl, they'll refill it
for you. That's the kind of place it is. Only trouble
is that I want to keep on eating and eating. It tastes
wonderful as it's going down. Every now and then
I noticed Julie looking at me. She was trying to
give me the old positive-thinking whammy. No
thank you. I wasn't having any tonight. We didn't
eat at Amana often. I'd be crazy to let such a chance
go by.

Two things happened at that meal. I ate too much. And Julie ate hardly anything at all. For the first time it began to percolate through my thick skull that Julie wasn't eating any meat. Come to think of it, I'd never noticed her eating meat. I wondered why. I saved that question to ask her when we were alone straightening up the barn. Oh yes, Dad discovered the mess I had left it in when I had emptied the wagon yesterday. As soon as we reached home, Dad ordered me to clean it up right now and he did mean right now.

So I did. I had no choice. Julie came along to help. And I asked her straight out. "How come, Julie, you didn't eat the meat today?"

"I never do, Barney. We do not eat meat in my country. We eat vegetables, fruits, grains, eggs and man-made food. But no meat."

"That's crazy," I said. "Meat's important. Everybody needs meat. My mom's a nut on nutrition and she urges me to eat meat."

"I do not think so," said Julie. "We are strong and healthy where I come from. But we do not eat meat. We feel all creatures have the right to life. Nobody kills or hurts a creature in my country. It is . . . it's barbaric."

"Thanks a lot," I said.

But I didn't mean it. How do you like that? This kid from nowhere calling me a barbarian? Made me want to smack her one. Talk about wild ideas. She was a wild one all right.

We finished the cleaning up in silence. Sometimes silence is good. Gives you time to think. And what I began to think was that Julie was beginning to seem fragile. Dad could call her wild. I could even call her ideas wild, but as I looked at her there I had a feeling that she was beginning to fade. Oh, not vanish. I don't mean something dumb like that. Only she was paler and thinner than I remembered her at first.

I mulled it over a bit. On the way back to the house, I burst out with my idea. Julie didn't act a bit surprised. "Yes, Barney," she said. "I do not think I have a long time to live. There are things one must do when one is in a negative country. I do not know what they are."

"I keep telling you," I burst in. "We are not a negative country."

This kid could get me angry in no time flat. First she calls us barbarians and next we are negative. Those are fighting words.

"You do not understand, Barney. But someday, you may," said Julie. "Let me explain. You see . . ."

But I didn't get to see, because Dad met us at the back porch and it would have been dumb to let Julie explain in front of him. I shushed her. But

I needn't have bothered. Dad never gave her a chance to speak. He had had a call from Bill Williams and was hunting us up to get the answers to some questions. I wasn't expecting more trouble, but that's what I got. Bill had given the metal weight to a physicist who had gotten so curious about the nature of the weight that he'd spent the day in the lab trying to pin down what metal it was. Holy cow! We were in for it now. Because Dad said they wanted to know exactly where we had found it.

"In the barn, Dad," I said. I was sticking to yesterday's story. "Regnad, Julie," I muttered in her direction. She kept her mouth shut.

Dad looked at me, thinking. "What was that, son?"

I knew he meant the regnad bit, but I played dumb. "In the barn, Dad, that's where we found the weights," I said. "Don't you remember? You told me they were there."

"Yes, I remember that all right. This is one of those weights?"

"Sure," I said.

And then drat! Julie did it. She had to go and do it. She said, "Not exactly, Mr. Sutton. A transmutation occurred. We were trying for gold, but we got . . . I do not know what."

"You two are standing there and telling me that

you changed lead into something else. Barney is this some more of your tom-foolery?" Dad stared at us. We stared back. What could we do or say that wouldn't get us in a thousand times more trouble? "I believe you mean it. I really think you mean it." Dad stood there fussing with his pipe, trying to get it lighted. And I knew why. It gave him time to think. "I do not understand it," said Dad. "Why is it that since Julie has come you find it necessary to make up these impossible lies. Perhaps Miss Bolen is right and Julie should go back to the state's care. I'll call her in the morning."

His last statement stunned me. I couldn't think for a moment. Let alone think positively. Julie's eyes got tears in them. Tears in yellow eyes are strange. But I mustn't think about that. I had to think positively. Don't send Julie back, Dad — that's what I was thinking.

Dad turned to go inside. I was feeling slightly frantic. "Think positively," I shouted, meaning it for Julie. "Think . . . think . . . think!"

Dad was halfway through the door. He turned back toward me. "I do not need you telling me how to think, young man," he snapped. "I will think however I wish . . ." He paused. "I suppose we had better let Julie stay until I have time to talk things over with your mother. I'll wait on the decision."

And he was gone. Julie and I gave out with a big sigh of relief. "We shall have to ride Diablo again," said Julie. "Tomorrow."

Right then I had an awful thought. What would happen after the gigantic meal I'd just put away and the snacks I'd been gobbling down. I was almost too heavy on that ride to Grandma's. I tried to explain this to Julie. But she wasn't about to let anything sidetrack her. Next morning, as soon as Dad left, we were in the barn. We dragged Diablo into place, put on our suits and then Julie started prowling around, hunting something. I couldn't figure out what. It dawned when she came toward me with a leather belt in her hand. She was about to rig up a seat belt for me. Good idea. I didn't object a bit.

Once I was strapped in place, the belt going across my legs and under Diablo's belly, Julie squeezed in between me and the pole, monkeyed with the dials on the transductor, and we were off. First came the ups and downs, then the wild circle motions and the blinding yellow light. My brain gave my mouth a nudge. "Julie," I whispered, "where are we going?"

"Mexico," came the answer . . . I started thinking *Mexico* with all my might. I could only hope Julie was pinpointing it a little more than that.

Which I guess she did. Because when we stopped we were in a wild and crazy spot . . . like a desert. There were cactus growing there. At least I think they were cactus. Some went straight up with lots of prickly arms reaching toward the sky. Some were round like balls and had needles sticking out every which way. And then there were things with fattish, thick pointed leaves growing in fields. I wondered who would want a crop of cactus.

I shifted my weight to get a look behind me and almost unhinged my jaw. It dropped open so far in surprise. Because behind us were pyramids. Honest to goodness pyramids. Holy cow! How had we ended up in Egypt? How great. I had always wanted to see the Egyptian pyramids.

Julie's whisper rustled in my ear. "I will get off and check," she said. "I think — I do not know — but I think perhaps I can speak enough Spanish to communicate. Diablo has taught me a little."

"How will knowing Spanish help you in Egypt?" I whispered back.

"Egypt?" I heard a giggle. "This is Mexico, Barney. Though I am not quite sure where. That I must find out."

"Are you getting a signal from your sensitizer?" I asked. After all . . . that's what we had come for, the escape hatch.

"No, nothing. That is why I must find out where we have landed, so we do not come back to the same area again."

"Better get your mask and helmet off," I said, "or you're going to scare these people to death."

"But of course," said Julie.

She did even more than that. She slipped off her shocking-pink jump suit as well and tossed it over Diablo's back, once again looking like a normal American girl in her blue jeans and sneakers. Then she carefully unscrewed his ear and removed the transductor. That was good thinking. I'd sure as heck hate to be taking off with that wild horse on my own.

Diablo and I were parked back of some building. From where I sat it could have been anything. I found out later it was a museum. For a while I watched Julie wandering about, talking to first one kid, then another. Then she disappeared from my view. It was taking her long enough. But it was worth it. At least that's what I thought when she reported back. She'd found out that these were the pyramids of Teotihuacán . . . that we were right outside of Mexico City . . . that there was a cave with a restaurant in it nearby which the children said we should try. But most important of all, that there was a legend about the pyramids. If you climbed the steps that led up to the top of the Pyramid of the Sun, and you climbed all the way without stopping, you would get your wish.

I pulled off my traveling gear in a big hurry. That climbing to the top was a great idea. The two of us hurried to the bottom of the steps. When I saw how

deep each step was and how high they went, I
thought it less of a great idea. I regretted my huge
Amana dinner all over again. The extra pounds
weren't going to help a bit. Julie took my hand and
gave it a squeeze. "Good luck," she said.

And she took off. Julie was so small and light
that she seemed to be skimming up the steps. My
movement was more like a heavy tank's. The first
dozen steps went along fine. And then my muscles
began to cramp, my breath got short, sweat began
popping out on my face. Man, oh, man it was hot!
But I plugged along. Nobody had said you had to
run up the thing to get your wish. And I was working at pacing my climb so I wouldn't have to give
up. I kept my eye on the step right ahead. Up with
the foot . . . up with the next . . . and the next
and the next. I felt like I was on a treadmill. I took
a quick glance backward. It was encouraging. The
steps went down a long way. I glanced up. I could
see Julie. She was already at the top, just sitting
there and waving me on.

So I kept at it. My breath was coming in spurts
that made my chest hurt. My knees were beginning to ache. I could hardly see. The sweat kept
dripping in my eyes. It was too much effort to get
an arm up to wipe them. Up . . . up . . . up . . .
three fourths of the way now. The top was closer.
And then . . . I was there.

"Ah, Barney. How wonderful. You made it. I knew you would. I did too. Now we will get our wishes."

"Holy cow!" I gasped. My words came out in spurts. "I forgot . . . to make . . . a wish."

"Perhaps your climb will help make my wish come true," said Julie.

"Nope," I said stubbornly. "I'll make one of my own."

So I did. I wished that Julie would get home safe. Okay, so it was probably the same as hers. But I wasn't going to let her boss me. I did it on my own.

I collapsed on the step next to her, exhausted. There was a buzzing in my head and my face was on fire. I hoped I wasn't going to do something stupid like faint. And I didn't. Why, after a while I even managed to get to my feet and look around. What a view. On one side was another pyramid. Julie said it was the Pyramid of the Moon. Mountains were off in the distance . . . smoke hung over another section. Maybe that's where Mexico City lay. Standing way up there I felt I could touch the clouds — a giant stride might take me to the sea. It was exciting.

Only you can't stand looking at scenery forever. When Julie suggested we go down, I was ready. And I was even more ready when she suggested we go and eat in the cave before taking off for home.

A sad thought hit. "How about money?" I asked.
"Do you not have any money with you?" asked
Julie.

My fingers felt in my pockets. I pulled out a
bunch of change. "I've got American money. But
this is Mexico," I said. With someone else I might
have said, "Stupid," but not to Julie.

"Good. They will take American money here.
Come on, Barney, we will go and try their tacos."

And away she went, hopping down the steps like
a grasshopper. I took my time. When she'd been
talking about this cave I had just assumed it was
right at hand. But no, we had to walk. After that
endurance climb, I was feeling pooped. Still, with
food promised at the end of the hike it was easier
to urge my legs forward. Anyway, we finally made
it. And whoever had told Julie about the spot was
a good friend. The cave was huge, all open across
one end. We walked in at the top and then twisted
down a mass of steps this way and that. There were
tables at different levels as we descended. I picked
a group near the top. Because my brain figured out
that we would have to go back up every step that
we were going down.

I slumped into a chair at an empty table, and Julie
slid very properly into one across from me. When
the waiter came up, I said nothing . . . just let
Julie do the talking. She must have done all right.
Because it only took the man a few minutes to come

back with cold pop and a plate of pancakes folded in half. Okay, so they weren't pancakes. But that's what they looked like. Turned out they were tortillas. You know, those flat corn cakes that they fold and fry in fat . . . makes them come out tasting like Fritos. But they don't stop there. They stuff them with things. Mine had lettuce and tomatoes and onion and ground beef. I took a quick look at Julie's. She had no meat. There were only two apiece and I could have eaten half a dozen without trying. My common sense took hold. If I was going to lose weight ever, I had to quit eating like a madman. So I bit in and ate slowly. They were great. I looked around and noticed other people putting on a relish that I spotted on our table too. It was a greenish-looking stuff. What I really wanted was ketchup. Ketchup makes anything better. But when you're in a foreign country, you should do as they do. So I did.

Holy Cow! I almost lost the inside of my mouth. My eyes bulged out. My tongue was on fire. Talk about hot. They must have made that relish with liquid fire. I couldn't swallow Coke fast enough to drown the heat. Julie was watching me, her eyes sort of big, startled. Then she began to giggle.

"I am sorry, Barney. I forgot to tell you. The sauce is hot," she said.

"Hot . . . That stuff isn't hot," I said. "It's hotter

than hot. I think they've found a new weapon. Instant fire."

Now I had a problem. My second taco was doused with that sauce too. Was I going to leave it and be hungry? Or eat it and die? I ate it. The things a guy will do just to stay alive are amazing.

My tongue felt numb all the way back to the museum and Diablo. We were sauntering along, in no special hurry, until we noticed the crowd of kids that were gathering in that general area. And we knew why . . . instantly. Diablo Grande. The kids had spotted Diablo. I had thought I couldn't possibly run any more that day. But I did. So did Julie. When we got there, I bet there were fifty kids gathered around, patting the horse, putting their fingers between his teeth, tugging on his tail. As soon as they spotted us, they were on us like a swarm of bees, holding little clay figures out toward us and yelling things like "you buy" . . . "originale" . . . "plenty cheap."

I couldn't resist. Neither could Julie. I spent every bit of money I had. Not that I thought for a minute that they were original stuff once buried there. You don't get great art for ten cents apiece. But I liked them.

When we finally got ourselves disentangled from all their grabbing hands, Julie and I began pulling on our suits. We couldn't travel without them and the kids weren't about to leave. So we dressed in front of them. What else could we do? They were a silent crowd . . . all eyes . . . staring . . . staring. I stuck the little figures on top of my head and pulled on my helmet. So did Julie. And then it happened. Trouble again. Some dumb tourists came by and spotted us, sitting there on Diablo. For some reason they seemed to have the idea that this was part of the museum's display. I ask you, what would a merry-go-round horse be doing in an area famous for its old Indian artifacts? The man unlimbered his camera and the two women were chattering to each other about the cute children and our funny costumes — how quaint we were. Couldn't those dopes tell that we weren't Mexicans: me with blond hair and Julie with her white skin and slanty yellow eyes? I suppose people see what they expect to see and come to think of it, it wasn't much. But what they saw next they didn't expect.

On account of Julie turned toward me and said, "We must go. Quickly. Snap on your mask."

Which I did. And bedlam broke loose. You'd have thought Frankenstein and Dracula had both appeared. The kids began screaming. The tourists were hollering something. Don't ask me what because Julie was whispering in my ear, "Think *home*."

And I did. The bouncing began. Suddenly I remembered. My seat belt. I hadn't fastened my seat belt. By the end of the third circle, I didn't even have hold of the belt. I hung on to the brass pole like I was frozen to it. And I thought *home* with all the strength of my think box. The blinding light came — the feeling of nothingness. And then it happened.

I was slipping. Diablo was tipping backward. Naturally, since I weighed so much I kept going back, slowly, slowly. I prayed I could hold on until we made the barn. But I didn't. I was off in free flight. I flailed the air with my arms and found myself doing somersaults. I flapped my hands like a bird and straightened out. Good-bye, Mom. Good-bye, Dad, I thought. Then splash! I had landed in water. How lucky can you get?

In a moment I surfaced. And here came trouble again. The lake patrol. Holy cow! I had landed in our lake, the one right near our house. But you can't swim in our lake except at the beach. It's against the law. I knew what was going to happen. I was about to be arrested. Oh, help! What would Dad say to that? I jerked the face mask off and tread water. The ranger turned his boat motor off so he could lecture me better.

"Well, son, what do you think you are doing?"

I knew what I was doing all right. So did he. I was swimming. How could I stay afloat without swimming? But I knew better than to get smart. "I'm . . . I . . . I fell in," I said. "I'm trying to get to shore."

"You just happened to be wearing that wet suit, I suppose, just in case you happened to fall in." He was sarcastic all right.

"No, sir, this is a jump suit," I said. "For flying. Only I started slipping and the horse threw me."

He looked at me as if I'd gone crazy. "Are you trying to tell me that when you go horseback riding you wear a suit for flying? Come on, kid. What's the joke?"

"If you knew this horse," I said, "you'd know how often you end up flying," I said. "I sure am sorry, officer. I didn't mean to land in the lake."

I guess the ranger had never heard an excuse

quite like mine. He sat there trying to make up his mind whether to fine me or let me go. I did the only possible thing. I thought positively. "Let me go. Let me go."

"I'll let you go, son," he said finally, "but I want your name. I think your folks should know about this and keep you from riding your horse into the lake."

I opened my mouth to tell him that the horse hadn't been in the lake. I shut it fast. I was getting tired. I wished he'd do something. "What's your name, son?"

I hated to tell him. But I did. "Barney," I said. "Barney Sutton."

"Okay, Barney. I'll let you off with a warning this time. But you end in the lake again and I'll see you get a stiff fine." He jerked on his motor's cord and it roared into action.

I paddled listlessly toward shore. The least the guy could have done, I thought, was to have given me a lift in. But maybe if I did a little positive thinking on myself, I could make it. And I did.

9 Positive Thinking Meets Its Match

WOULDN'T YOU KNOW, the ranger called Dad that very night to tell him about my swimming in the lake and how I said that I'd been thrown there by a horse and how I claimed to wear a jump suit whenever I went riding. You know the stuff he reported. So Dad got angry at me, about as angry as I'd ever seen him. He bombarded me with words about my wild fabricating of stories — that's what he called it. He flatly accused me of lying about riding a horse when I was caught swimming. He put me down proper like. I was exhausted when he had finished. So was he.

I was moving toward the stairs and bed when he asked the fatal question. "And where, may I ask, was Julie while all this was going on?"

If I'd had my brain cut in, I'd have said I didn't know which would have been the truth, at least part of it. Only I said, I supposed she was on

Diablo. Then I could have bitten my tongue off.

"Diablo? Diablo? That means the devil, doesn't it? It's Spanish," said Dad.

"Could be," I said. "He acts like that sometimes."

"We are not speaking of the devil himself, are we?" Dad was very intent, his eyes dared me to dream up another lie. And here I was so out of practice I couldn't come up with anything. And I needed a good lie at the moment. So what did I do? I told the truth. "Diablo is a horse," I said.

"I was waiting for that," said Dad. "The horse that threw you in the lake no doubt?"

"Yes sir." The words didn't come out loud and clear. I could only whisper.

"The horse that you fell off of or that threw you into the lake or some such nonsense?" Dad was zeroing in on our secret. I was trapped.

"Yes . . ." I thought a moment. "At least that's the way I think it was. Julie and me, we were together. Only I'm pretty heavy — I ate too much at Amana, Dad. I've got to watch that. You know I'd lost almost fifteen pounds, but yesterday's dinner and all the crackers the night before, it cut down on that loss some." I was stalling for time.

"I wondered what was happening to your clothes," said Dad. "You are to go into town with me tomorrow afternoon and get some new jeans. You can wait at the library for me and I'll drive you out after my class."

"How about Julie?" I asked. "We can't go off and leave Julie."

"It will be good for you and Julie to be separated for a few hours. Ever since that girl has come, you are a changed person. And the change has not been an improvement — making horrendous concoctions in the basement, hitchhiking into town, swimming in the lake. I tell you, Barney, I have reached the end of my tolerance. That child must go. And when Miss Bolen comes tomorrow, I will tell her just that."

"You mean that sweet-talking blond witch is coming?"

Dad interrupted me sternly. "Barney!" The way he said it stopped me cold. "I will not have you talk of an adult in that way, a professional person trying to do her job. I admit she is annoying, but nevertheless her diagnosis of Julie was correct. She is wild, undisciplined, a liar and a show-off. I think the amnesia story is a fabrication of her clever little mind. I, for one, am going to see that she is taken care of by people who know how to deal with disturbed minds."

Dad turned and stalked into his study. He slammed the door so hard behind him that my ears bent back from the sound. Julie came running. I wondered how much she had heard. Her eyes had a kind of glint . . . yellow can do that. But she looked sad.

"Mr. Sutton is, I believe, very angry." She whispered the words. "He is angry at me."

"Not exactly." Whispers fit my mood. I whispered too. "He's mostly angry at me. And all because I fell in the lake. Big deal! You'd have thought I murdered somebody, the way he went on. And then there was the horse bit."

"What horse bit . . . you were bitten, Barney?" asked Julie.

"Not that kind of bit, not biting. It means my horse story. Dad thinks I'm horsing around." I said it and saying it made me snort. Joking helps sometimes. "See, I told the ranger about being tossed in the lake by a horse. I wasn't thinking. It just came out."

"But that was the truth," said Julie.

"Julie, girl," I said, "I've told you and told you and told you. The truth can sometimes turn out to be your enemy. Believe me."

"I cannot believe that. The truth sets people free. I've seen that in your books. It opens the spirit, it is beautiful," said Julie.

"Okay, Julie. That's great sounding," I said. "But in our world . . . it doesn't always work out that way. You keep your idea. I'll hold to mine. But that beautiful truth of mine made Dad decide to send you back to the home. What will we do, Julie?"

"Perhaps I will take Diablo and leave," she said.

"Holy cow, Julie, that would really land me in a mess! With the reputation I'm beginning to get around here, they'd think I'd murdered you. Don't just disappear. Promise?"

"I could leave a note . . . Oh, all right, Barney, I promise. Something will turn up. I have this feeling. After all, I ran all the way to the top of that pyramid without stopping and I know my wish is coming true."

I didn't want her to leave, but as I stood there looking at her I had this crazy feeling that she was getting transparent . . . Julie was failing fast. I gave her hand a squeeze. "I hope your wish comes true, Julie. I do. And mine too."

Early next afternoon Dad whisked me off to town to do some shopping. On my way over to the library, I stopped off to ask Bill Williams about the weight and could I please have it back now. I expected him to just hand it to me. Well, I had thought wrong. He began quizzing me about where I'd found it, had I seen more? I gave stingy answers, hoping that would end it all.

"Could I please have the weight now, Bill?" I asked.

"As a matter of fact," said Bill, "I don't have it. But tell you what, Barney, I'll get in touch with your dad this afternoon. There's been an interesting development I need to discuss with him. Okay?"

I could see I didn't have any choice. "Okay," I said glumly. "I guess so."

But I had a gnawing worry growing at the back of my mind. What was wrong with that weight? Why was everyone so mysterious? I forgot my worries when I settled down to my reading. It had taken some time to find, but I'd finally hunted down material about transmutations and power conductors. I had to work so hard to understand the words that I didn't hear Dad speak my name. I wasn't even aware he was there until his hand grabbed my shoulder.

"Hey, watch it," I said, thinking somebody was being funny. "Oh, hi, Dad, I didn't know it was you."

"What's proving so interesting, son?" He leaned over to take a look. "When did you get interested in that kind of stuff?"

"Since Julie came," I said. "Gosh, Dad, I've learned heaps."

"And not all of it good by a long shot," muttered Dad. "Come on, Barney."

We hardly spoke to each other in the car going home. I resented his remarks about Julie. And Dad? I don't know what he was upset about. I didn't much care. When we pulled into the yard, my stomach gave a lurch. There was Miss Bolen's car at the back porch. I had this feeling of urgency. Julie needed help. I was out of the car and into the house in record time. And I was right. Oh, I was so right. Julie and Miss Bolen were standing in the living room having a staring match. "I won't go. I won't go." That's what Julie was saying. She was saying it whispery like, but no one could doubt her determination. And Miss Bolen was standing there smiling, smiling! I wanted to wipe it right off her face.

"I am afraid, child, that you have no choice. The decision is made. Please go up and get your things. Dr. Sutton needs to sign a few papers."

At which point Dad came in. I wondered what had happened to positive thinking. Julie hadn't made much headway with Miss Bolen. I concentrated on Dad. And what I was thinking was "Don't let her do it. Don't let her take Julie, Dad."

He stood there looking at us all. It was dramatic. You could feel the tenseness in the air. "Good afternoon, Miss Bolen," said Dad.

"Ah, Dr. Sutton. I was just telling Julie that you had to sign the release papers indicating that you had turned the child over to me. I am afraid she is not very happy."

I had a feeling that Miss Bolen was feeling triumphant. She may not have understood why she had left Julie the last time, but she sure as heck wasn't going to do it again. We were sunk. Still, I kept at Dad's thinking . . . "Don't let her, Dad . . . don't let her." I sent out those words, desperately. Maybe Julie caught the idea. Or maybe I was staring at Dad so hard that my eyes led her to understand what I was thinking. But Dad, who had been telling me only a half hour before that he was going to send Julie back, suddenly said, "I wonder, Miss Bolen, if this is wise. I find with children, and adults too, that it is better to inform them ahead of time about an unpleasant action. Especially if there is resistance to the idea. I fear nothing would be gained by moving her today."

"That may be, Dr. Sutton. That may be. But I find it better to do an unpleasant job instantly instead of postponing it. I do not enjoy such confrontations as this. The decision is made."

The heck she didn't enjoy the scene. She was glorying in it. I hated the woman. But there was no point wasting energy on that. "Don't let her, Dad. Don't let her, Dad," I thought.

I was concentrating so hard I didn't even hear the phone ringing. Not until that woman picked it up. She was pushy, that's for sure. It was for Dad. He talked along making surprised comments and we heard: "You don't say? . . . I had no idea . . . they are coming here? . . . Good heavens, Bill, I can't believe it . . . of course, I'll tell the children. Yes, they're right here. You want to see both of them . . . Together? I see . . . yes, of course, Bill."

He hung up. We looked at him, waiting. He

stood for a moment digesting what he had heard. When he spoke it was in his lecture tones: slow, each word clearly enunciated. "As we were saying, Miss Bolen, I think you must leave Julie here until the weekend at least."

"Really, Dr. Sutton . . ." Miss Bolen said.

He raised his hand to stop her interruption. "I have just talked with Bill Williams who reports that the find the children made last week of a metal weight is creating much excitement in scientific circles. So much, in fact, that two research men from Los Alamos, New Mexico, are coming to examine it. They have stipulated that they want to talk to the children — both of the children — and together. Now I think that if you are not willing to listen to reason, I shall get a court order."

"Reason . . . science . . . piffle!" snapped Miss Bolen. "Our only concern here is the child."

"I disagree," said Dad, who could get hoity-toity himself when someone ignored his logic. "I am not at all sure that you are actually considering Julie's welfare. You are much more concerned about your dignity. There seems to be an element of fear in your decision — the fear that you will lose face if you do not drag Julie back with you today. I cannot see that she is being harmed. I think Barney is suffering from the contact more than she. But in a situation like this, where science might benefit, I do not see that a few more days here can be devastating."

Jumping Jehoshaphat, Dad was sure laying it on thick. Did it help? Not a bit. Miss Bolen marched upstairs with a determined flounce just daring us to interfere. Since none of us had made a move, she was going to get Julie's things herself. Dad stood there a moment, then he took off after her. I knew we had lost. I was standing there, sunk in disgust.

"Barney, Barney," whispered Julie. "What is this . . . this Los Alamos . . . this New Mexico?"

"New Mexico? That's one of the states, out in the western part of the country. And Los Alamos is one of the places they do atom research. At least that's what I think they're doing."

I turned toward Julie and I felt as if someone had given me a punch in the stomach. Julie was standing there, hands clasped together, an expression on her face of such sheer joy that I couldn't grasp what was happening. Holy cow, what had I said? *What* had I said?

"New Mexico . . . Los Alamos." She said the words over like they were a magic formula. "Of course, now I remember . . ."

"The escape hatch," I said. "That's where it is, isn't it?"

She nodded. "Come, Barney. We go now before they come back." Which was a great idea. It would

be a bit rough on me when I got back from Los
Alamos without Julie, but it was the only way to
save the kid. What the heck, a guy had to take
chances now and then.

I grabbed her hand. Me, Barney Sutton, grabbing a girl's hand? Shows how much I'd changed
in the last weeks. We were halfway across the yard
when we heard Dad's voice and Miss Bolen's in a
shrieking chorus. They were calling our names.

"Don't stop! Don't stop!" gasped Julie.

But I couldn't help myself. I did. And since I
had a good firm grip on Julie, she stopped too.
"Listen," I said, as Miss Bolen came toward us like
a bulldozer. "Listen, we didn't have time to get
set up. And if they had found Diablo, we might
have been in trouble. Agreed?"

She nodded.

"You'll simply have to figure out a way to get
back here," I said.

Which turned out to be easier than I had thought.
Miss Bolen told us that she and Dad had reached
an agreement, that she would bring Julie back when
the scientists arrived. She didn't sound very happy
about her decision, but with all of us staring at her,
she didn't have a chance to change her mind. I
could only hope she wouldn't change it after she
got Julie back to the home. From here on, it was
up to the kid from another country.

Julie was very polite as she left. She shook hands

with me. Then she went and shook hands with Dad. "I think you are right that I should see the gentlemen from Los Alamos. I will be most interested to talk to them. Talking to scientists is almost like being at home."

"No kidding?" I said.

"What an amazing child," said Dad.

Miss Bolen was too busy getting Julie's suitcase and Julie into the car to say anything. Which left me feeling strangely sad, like I felt when my pup died of distemper. Dad and I walked back toward the porch after the car had left. "You know, Dad, you can count on one thing," I said.

"What's that, Barney?" he asked, tamping away at the tobacco in his pipe.

"Julie's not like other girls, not at all. And if she said she likes scientists why then she likes talking to scientists. Because that kid always tells the truth."

"That wild one?" asked Dad. "Oh, come now, Barney."

I shrugged my shoulders and gave up. How mixed up could grownups get about a person? I kind of wished Dad knew Julie the way I did.

10   Questions, Questions, Questions

I<small>F</small> I was wondering what I'd do with my time now
that Julie was gone, I needn't have worried. Dad
kept me going at full speed. Ugh! He could dream
up some dillies in the job line, like cleaning and
scrubbing the basement where we'd dropped the
gunk from the copper boiler and straightening out
the mess we'd left in the loft. I liked the last job.
Every now and then I'd climb down and give Diablo
a pat and maybe dream a bit. It's funny. If I caught
a casual glimpse of Diablo as I worked, he looked
like any other wildly plunging, wooden merry-go-
round horse. But when I'd think of the trips I had
made on his back, zooming into the wild blue yon-
der, I realized how things aren't always what they
seem.

One thing about the work, it gave me plenty of
time to dig into my memory for snatches of things
that Julie had told me about her land, her people.

I remembered her talking about nobody eating meat or fish — some didn't even eat vegetables because of their deep respect for life, all life. Most of their food was created in laboratories. I remembered her describing the way her people lived in small communities, each in his own home, and that each community governed itself, except for the schools. Kids all went to schools — on what sounded to me like college campuses — from the moment they could toddle. And they progressed at their own rate. At some time she had mentioned that people had to work to earn the privilege of voting — that was an idea to chew on — and how there were no wars or hunger or enemies or hatred. It all sounded unbelievable to me.

The word enemy made me think about Bill Williams. It's crazy how I had always thought of Bill as a friend. But now I wasn't sure at all. And right in the midst of that humdinger of a thought, Dad called me for lunch. I didn't hurry. Lunch with Dad was anything but exciting. He usually read some report or book as he ate. So that started me thinking of Julie again and how she liked to chatter. What was it she'd said about positive and negative worlds? But before I could get the idea into focus, I had reached the table and just bitten into my peanut butter sandwich when Dad began talking. And it was queer, not only was he talking but he gave off a kind of excitement. It startled me. Hardly had I begun to wonder why, when I had the answers.

First off, Mom was coming home — and on Saturday, which was only three days off. I let out a yip at that news. Such a loud yip that Mr. Snodhopper eating dinner a mile away at his farmhouse probably heard the echo. Oh, boy! How great . . . Mom coming home. It's not that I dislike hamburgers and TV dinners and peanut butter. But even your favorite foods get pretty dull when you have them continuously. I'd hardly recovered from the first news when Dad handed me a second. The Los Alamos scientists were coming. And wouldn't you know, they were coming on Saturday morning too.

That news really hit me. I knew right quick that it meant I couldn't go along with Dad to meet Mom. I'd have to settle for a talk fest with Julie and the scientists instead.

I'll say this for Saturday. It wasn't dull. Miss Bolen dropped Julie off about ten in the morning. The kid kept tossing her head with a wild nervous jerk like you do when you're trying to contain a wild burst of excitement. And yet she seemed so frail that I was afraid if I sneezed in her direction I'd knock her flat. I had this awful feeling inside that we didn't have much time.

Bill Williams arrived about an hour after Julie, bringing along the two physicists. I had a hard time getting their names. I finally caught on that the lean and lanky one was Hank something or other and the solid, intense guy was Melvin.

We sat down properly in the library, Julie perching on a chair as if she were poised to make a run for Diablo. Okay! I was ready. The men settled down deliberately like they were ready to make a whole day's job of the interview. Dad stayed only a moment. He had hardly said hello when he was saying good-bye so he could set off for the airport. I think maybe he had the idea that a little positive thinking on his part might bring Mom's plane in ahead of time. Turned out it didn't help. Mom was hours late.

So there we were in the library. Bill Williams held out the lead weight. I was glad to see he was finally going to let us have it back. Julie took it. Then, not knowing exactly what to do with it, she handed it back to me. I took a good tight grip on it. They weren't going to get it back in their hands again if I could help it.

"Suppose we start at the beginning," said Bill. "Where did you find this weight?"

"In our barn," I answered quickly. That was the truth.

"In your barn," said Melvin. He made me nervous. Like it was some kind of police interrogation and we were spies or worse. "You are sure you found this in the barn? Very sure?"

"Yes, sir." Julie and I both whispered the answer. We were nervous. The whispers seemed to bother the men. It made me grin inside.

"Come, come, children," said Hank. "You surely understand the seriousness of this."

"No, sir," I whispered. It gave me great twinges of excitement to see how the whispers bugged him. Maybe it was dumb, but they were acting officious. I like to bug officious people. "No, sir," I whispered on. "Because we can't figure out what all the excitement's about. I mean, here's this plain little old weight . . ."

"See here, young man," exploded Melvin. "That is not a plain old ordinary weight. It is something entirely new — the metal is. One we've never seen

before. It is heavier than uranium — that we could
test. The components are fascinatingly near those
of uranium, but not quite. Obviously this metal is
not in its natural state. Someone has shaped it into
a weight, the kind of weight that might be used
on a scale."

"Oh, yes, it's a weight all right," I said.

"Let's get back to your finding it in the barn," said
Hank. "We're puzzled about why you took the
weight to a jeweler . . . to Bill Williams here."

Julie looked at me. I looked at Julie. What were
we going to do? Telling the truth was going to lead
to some mighty complicated questions. Dodging
the truth could make even more difficulties because
one little misstep and we'd get ourselves trapped.

So we sat there like dummies, staring at each other.

"Come, come, Barney," said Bill. "It's not like you to be so quiet."

"I don't know what to tell you," I said. And that was the exact truth.

Suddenly the last thing in the world I expected to happen happened. Hank began talking to us like Julie and me were people — not some nuts or weirdos, but people.

"Look, kids," he said, leaning back and pulling out a pipe. You could see him relaxing. "We're so darned excited about this discovery of yours that we're after the facts like a bird dog on the trail of a pheasant. We're scaring you to death with our intenseness. Sorry about that. But I can tell you this, that piece of metal you found is so new, so important that someday kids just like you may be reading about your discovery in history books, like they read about Einstein and Ptolemy. Now, what we want you to do . . ." He struck a match and paused ". . . is to start at the beginning and tell it as it was. We're going to try to hold ourselves in and not interrupt you. But now and then we may break in with a question. When scientists come across something as exciting as this, you've got to expect them to pop questions at you. Okay?"

Julie looked at me. I looked at Julie. She gave her head a weak imitation of a wild toss. That worried me. But I'd think about it later. "I think we should do as they suggest," she whispered. "I think we should, Barney. The truth is the only way."

"See here, Barney," said Bill and his voice had a sharp edge to it, "have you been playing one of your little tricks on me again?"

I shook my head. How could a guy as nice as Bill have turned into a full-size YUCK. Maybe I wasn't so good at recognizing enemies myself. But before I could get my mouth into gear, Julie was talking. Whispering, really. The men leaned forward, straining to get each word.

"It's all very simple," she said. "Barney and I wanted to try an experiment. We thought it might be fun to see if we could turn lead into gold. Barney said he'd never tried anything like that before."

"You've got to be kidding," said Bill. His face was frozen in horror.

"Kidding? Kidding?" Julie thought a moment. "Oh, no, sir, I am truthing. It is the only way."

"Not truthing, Julie," I said. "Telling the truth. Here people call it telling the truth."

"Did you note that, Hank? The girl is not from here, whatever that means," muttered Melvin.

Julie kept on. "Thank you, Barney. Sometimes I get things mixed up, sirs. I am telling the truth. That is what I am doing. Barney and I found the necessary chemicals and mixed them up. They are simple elements so they are easy to find. I was not sure I could remember all of the formula, but I tried."

"You know a formula?" said Melvin. He had stopped taking notes and sat staring.

Julie turned toward him. "Oh, yes, sir. I know many formulas. My father is a teacher of science and he is, how do you say it, strict. Always he stresses accuracy. In measuring a formula it is of the utmost importance."

"You don't say," said Melvin. For some crazy reason he sounded angry.

"But, of course, I say. Because it is true. I have certain problems with the formula . . ."

"I bet," said Melvin, sarcastic like.

"Because . . ." Julie was trying to keep going, but the doubt and distrust being generated in the room was unnerving ". . . because I had to change the proportions of the chemicals, change from positive to negative, you see. In my country we do not change lead into gold. We change gold into lead. It is more valuable."

"Oh, my aching head," muttered Bill.

"The kid is nuts, nuts or an actress," said Melvin.

Only Hank seemed to be listening. Really listening. "So you were going to try to change lead into gold. Is that what you are saying?" he asked.

"Yes, do you not do that here?" asked Julie.

"Not since the Middle Ages," said Hank. "But

go on, your ingenuity is fascinating. You had the chemicals ready — then what?"

"We needed some lead," I said, interrupting. "And we couldn't find any. So we asked Dad and he remembered seeing an old scale in the barn and suggested we might see if the weights were lead."

"Barney and I had an awful time looking for the weights, because of the storm and the barn has no lights. But after we had hunted awhile, why there they were. And they were lead and . . ." She paused.

Heck! She had every reason to stop dead. The expressions on the listeners' faces would have stopped a buffalo stampede. They looked fierce, doubting, disgusted. Julie waited a moment, not knowing whether to stop or go on. Being a girl, she went on.

"You see, there were five weights, but they were too heavy for us to carry all of them. It was beginning to rain hard and we had to run. We took only three. That's all we could manage and still run."

"And you put them in the chemicals and presto," said Bill.

He shouldn't have said it like that. His voice, his words all shouted *liar*. I could feel my face getting red. But Julie never hesitated.

"Oh, no sir, Mr. Williams . . ."

"Can't you speak louder?" said Hank. "I feel like

we're all in some cavern or wire-tapped room. Talk louder, girl."

"I am sorry. When we are transducting, we must whisper because the transceiver is so delicate. I forgot that I did not need to whisper."

Inside I groaned. The kid was cutting her throat — no, both our throats. But I didn't know how to help her. So I kept quiet. "Did you hear that? Did you hear that?" Bill was really excited. "The kid's been watching science fiction movies. Transducted . . . transceivers. *Transbaloney!*" he said.

Speaking in a very normal tone, Julie said calmly, "Things you do not understand, sir, are not necessarily made up or wrong."

Ever seen a man explode? For a moment there I thought we were all about to be peppered with bits of muscle, blood, skin . . . little pieces of Bill Williams. He was angry, so angry that he turned black, then purple, then red.

"Did you hear that? Did you hear the little pipsqueak. Why for two cents . . . no, for nothing, I'd . . . I'd . . ."

"Mr. Williams," said Hank in a level, stern tone, "we are conducting a scientific investigation. Emotional reactions like yours have no place in such an interview. Perhaps you had best wait outside if you cannot control yourself. I sense there is something strange here, some truth. But with you shouting about, I'll never recognize it. Get out or shut up. Which is it to be?"

Bill shut up. Julie went on. "Once we had the lead, we also needed an energy conductor. Chemicals are not enough."

"Very interesting," said Melvin, writing like mad. "How did she know that?"

"And we used this transductor. It is very old, but it did work," said Julie, "what with the storm and all."

"Go on. Go on," said Hank. "What then?"

"I think," said Julie," that somehow we connected with the lightning force and changed it into the energy we needed through the electrical system. A generator blew at the power plant."

"She's right. She's exactly right," said Bill. "It took twelve hours to repair a damaged generator. Imagine her having enough imagination to tie the generator to this. Remarkable imagination."

But Bill's remarks didn't discourage Hank. Instead they seemed to act like a revelation. "H'mmmmm," he said, "maybe they did manage something. Maybe the lightning bolt did go through the chemicals. What force that would generate!"

Julie plowed on. "With the lights out, it was very dark and Mr. Sutton said we must go to bed. In the morning the weights were the way you see them. No, that is not quite correct. They had a heavy crust of black carbon on them. Barney and I sanded the black off of this small weight and took it to Mr. Williams. Barney said Mr. Williams was a good friend and could tell us if we had actually achieved a transmutation. But Mr. Williams examined it and said it was not gold. He kept the weight so that he could find out what the metal really was."

And then Julie got this funny look on her face — kind of pleased and surprised all at once. "But, of course . . ." she whispered. "Of course! Now I know what it is."

"You do?" Melvin and Hank shouted it together. The sound was so loud, that darned if Julie didn't tumble off her chair. I told you she was getting fragile. While they were helping her up, someone said, "Out of the mouths of babes," and another said, "What will they think of next?"

"Regnad . . . regnad . . ." I whispered between sounds.

"What was that, Barney?" asked Bill. "What did you say?"

Jumping Jehoshaphat! That man was a king-sized pain. I turned away from him. Poor Julie. With Hank and Melvin begging her to tell them what she thought the metal was, Bill voicing his sarcastic doubts and me whispering regnad, she didn't know what to do. She turned back and forth, looking at Hank, then at Bill, then at me . . . her eyes had a wild, trapped look.

"Oh, go on," I said at last. "Tell them. It couldn't make any difference now."

"It's tuminium," said Julie.

"Say that again," said Hank. "Or better still, spell it."

So Julie did. They chewed the word over in their minds. "Where do you find tuminium?" asked Hank.

"It's quite common in our country. We use it as our prime energy source. When the atoms of this mineral are smashed, there is no dangerous ash or residual material."

Melvin looked like he was going to faint or maybe throw up. He couldn't digest the idea that this little, frail, black-haired girl could be spouting all this scientific stuff. So okay, it is unusual. But just because she sounded like an advanced physics text didn't mean she was a nut. And that's the way Hank and Bill were looking at her . . . like she was an escapee from some juvenile booby hatch. Inside I was chuckling. Wouldn't they get a jolt if they knew where she'd really come from. Which sent me off thinking on my own. Julie had hinted at her world, but come to think of it, I didn't know where it was either.

And while I was worrying this thought, I heard Hank asking Melvin, "Do you think some country has discovered a new metal? Perhaps Russia?"

"Doesn't seem possible," said Melvin. "Still, it's dangerous not to consider every possibility. The weight had to come from some place . . ." He left it hanging there.

And then a brilliant idea hit me. It could solve Julie's problem. Whether it solved the scientists' problem didn't trouble me a bit. "Hey . . . Hey!"

Everyone looked at me. Good, I had their attention. "Why don't Julie and I go and get the other weights for you. The lead ones and the ones like this one. You could compare them. How about it?"

"Good idea," said Hank. "I'll give you a hand."

"No, no," I said. "If you want to see them, you'll have to let us do it ourselves. It will take some time. Okay?" I grabbed Julie's hand and stood waiting.

"Okay," said Hank reluctantly. But at least he had said it. Melvin only nodded his head.

As we were going out the door, I heard Bill saying, "But you don't know that kid like I do. He's the champion prankster of the town. Why, I remember . . ."

I cringed at the kind of dumb thing he might be telling them. But not for long. Julie looked delicate but she could sure put on the speed. It took everything I had to keep up with her. Once inside the barn, I pulled the door shut and then gave Julie a hand with Diablo. We had him and the pole in place in record time. Without a word, we grabbed our jump suits, pulled them on and clambered onto Diablo's back.

"Think!" came Julie's whisper in my ear.

I was busy pulling on my helmet. I fumbled with the strap. When you're in a hurry, fingers can get all twisted up. I barely had it tightened and was working on the mask when we began bouncing.

"Think . . ."

And I thought. I thought *New Mexico* and, just to pinpoint it a bit, I thought *Los Alamos*. Made sense to me that the escape hatch had to be near the atomic research center. Diablo's bouncing got wilder and wilder, the circle whirled faster, faster, faster until everything was spinning in a mass of golden light. I shut my eyes and grasped the brass pole with all my strength. Jumping Jehoshaphat! I sure hoped I didn't slide off this time. There wasn't much water between Iowa and New Mexico and I could imagine the kind of hole I'd make plunging down into solid earth from this height.

I felt a sharp pain in my ears from pressure, my brain was reeling. Diablo's up and down motions began to slow. I opened my eyes. There we were. Right in the barn as usual. I had a moment of panic. Holy cow, what a mess we'd be in if we were really still sitting in the barn at home. But you can't wait forever to find out bad news. I tugged open the door and whistled in relief. Wherever we were, it wasn't home, that was for sure.

11 The Blow Up

JULIE UNDERSTOOD my whistling exhaust, because quick as a buttered eel she was off Diablo and holding my hand. I could feel her trembling. The kid was really excited. Well, she had nothing on me. I was excited too. Wow, what a wild, desolate-looking place we had landed in. I looked behind me to check on Diablo and saw the barn had faded away. Behind the horse was a rough outcropping of rock — farther on there were trees, like aspens and pines. And off in the distance were the mountains. We stood there soaking in the view, and mainly I was wondering . . . wondering whether this was New Mexico. I had this strange sinking feeling in my stomach that maybe we had landed on the moon.

"It is here . . . it is here . . . we are very close," whispered Julie. "Come. Let's go."

"You're kidding, it can't be. The transmuter can't

be in such a desolate place. A machine needs cover of some sort. Where would it be?"

"I do not know," said Julie, "but the sensitizer in my skin will guide us. Oh, do hurry, Barney. Don't just stand there."

I didn't stand. Heck no. The way Julie was moving I had to run to keep up. And with the rocky, uneven ground, I was doing one of those exhausting balancing acts, trying to stay on my feet. I didn't believe her. Not really. But I couldn't let her go wandering around with rattlesnakes and gila monsters and stuff like that lurking around. It was hard work being noble.

But imagine my surprise. I actually caught up with Julie. She pulled off her mask and bent over gasping. Her skin had a peculiar bluish tinge. She looked awful. And a terrible fear began gnawing inside me. I began some positive thinking on my own. "Let her make it. Please, let her make it," I thought.

"Come on, Julie, I'll give you a hand. You point the way," I said, grabbing her arm.

There were tears in her eyes. "Oh, Barney," she whispered. And pointed. I stared at where she was pointing. Holy cow! A cave. Halfway up a rough cliff was a dark opening. That made sense. A cave would be hidden, dry, secret. It was going to be tough going to get there, but I had this surge of determination. We were going to get there. It was something I simply had to do. And I did. I half dragged, tugged, pushed to move her along. It was lucky Julie was so lightweight. At the altitude we were working, even the littlest extra effort can be exhausting.

And then I could feel Julie's hand tensing. She stopped. "You must wait here," she said. "There is a shield guarding the entrance. I must do this on my own." I didn't need any urging to wait. I plunked down where I was and watched her as she stood in front of the dark opening. I have no idea what she did. But in a few minutes, the bright pink suit was gone. I sat there waiting, a little numb inside. Too much had been happening.

And then I was swamped in light, a blue-white light, the kind of light a million flashbulbs might make if they went off at once. I squinched my eyes to watch. She was taking off without saying good-bye. Only I was wrong.

She came through the light like a bouncing pink ball. How great to see her with some of her old wild spirit. "Oh, Barney, Barney, it's here, it's here! It takes a few minutes to activate. Perhaps even a little longer because I do not believe anyone has used it for a long time."

I thought she had a safe bet there. "Barney?" Julie reached out and grabbed my hand. I couldn't believe it. She was looking sad. Not happy at all. She stood staring at me with those great yellow eyes.

I felt dizzy. "Barney, come with me. My world is such a happy place. You would love it. I know you would. My parents would welcome you. They have always longed for a son. And I would have a brother. Please come, Barney."

"Hey," I grumbled. "None of that positive thinking now. I have to make up my own mind."

We stood staring at each other. Julie broke the spell with a giggle and there's nothing quite like a giggle to break up something serious. She gave her head a toss, one of those wild, neck-stretching tosses. Like Diablo.

"You do not understand about positive thinking, Barney. It cannot interfere with an individual's own feelings of rightness. Don't you see, I can't make you do anything that you feel is wrong. Remember Miss Bolen. We influenced her the first time, because she had doubts about her action. But we couldn't change her mind the second time because she was convinced she was right."

"So that was it," I said, kind of thinking out loud. "I'd wondered about that . . . why it hadn't worked."

I pulled myself to my feet. Julie grabbed my arm. "Do come, Barney."

"I can't pop off like that," I said slowly. "What would the folks do? I mean after all, I'm their only son too and they're used to having me around."

"Then it's good-bye," said Julie. "Remember me,

Barney, sometimes." She pulled on her mask. The light was getting fiercely bright and a high-pitched whining shrilled from the cave. Julie turned to go.

"Hey, Julie. Wait . . . Wait. I've a million things to ask you. How do I get home?"

"Jumping Jehoshaphat!" Julie grinned at me when she said it. She slipped something in my hand. "I almost forgot the transductor. Screw it tightly into the right ear. It's set correctly."

The light swallowed her up. She was gone. "Hey, Julie," I whispered. I didn't dare blast her with a shout. The whining sounds were louder. "What's the name of your world. You never told me . . . Julie."

I heard her voice, but it was mixed up with the noises of a machine — whine, whisper, rasp. Whatever she said, I didn't have time to sort it out. There was a fantastic blue-white glow. The whine became so unbearable that I clapped my hands over my ears. And then a monstrous blast knocked me backward. The ground shook and I went head over heels down the hill. Beats climbing down, I suppose, but it gave me a rugged bunch of assorted bumps and bruises.

I lay where I had fallen for a while, resting and thinking. Then I got to my feet and stared back at the cave. It was faintly yellow now. But soon it faded to a dark nothingness. She was gone. I hoped she had made it. Oh, how I hoped. I turned and headed back for the spot where I had left Diablo. Halfway there I had a frightening thought. Where was the transductor? I let out a relieved breath. I was still clutching it in my hand, clutching it so hard in fact that the dials had made red spots in my palm. I only hoped I hadn't knocked something screwy when I fell. But there was no point standing there and looking at the dials. I'd never know whether they were set right or wrong. I started moving again.

It was lonely climbing on Diablo's back by myself. I missed Julie already. Carefully, I unscrewed the ear, got the transductor in place and the ear twisted back in. I felt awfully silly sitting out there in the midst of a wilderness on a merry-go-round horse. But it was pale in comparison to my feeling of helplessness at having no idea of the power source I was hooking into. Still, I had no choice. I had to try. I could imagine having to explain to my father how I had ended up at Los Alamos while he was at the airport getting Mom. I did the only thing I could. I adjusted my face mask and thought *home*. I thought the idea with all the power of my mind.

The barn took shape around me and the wild desert landscape became a blur as we began to bounce. But something was going wrong. Diablo's bounce was jerky, jigglety. We began moving in a circle. But I could tell it was an awfully lopsided circle. I was having a hard time holding on as we lurched from one side to the other. My stomach had prickles exploding in it. I was scared. The pace picked up. I thought *home* harder and harder, grabbed Diablo's mane with one hand and grasped the brass pole with the other. This wasn't like our other trips. And I knew it. Whatever power I had latched onto, it was sure erratic, coming and going in spurts. My eyes were blinded by yellow light. We were off. The light got more intense. Was Diablo's head turning red? *Home . . . Home* I thought in a jumble. It was the last conscious thought I had.

When I came to, I was lying out in a field. My head hurt. I must have landed on it. And whatever was under me sure felt prickly. I inched my way up on my elbow, holding my head. It hurt less with my hand under it. Things kept whirling around, out of focus. I managed to get on my knees. One idea came through loud and clear. I felt awful. I finally staggered to my feet. Holy cow! What had happened? The field was laid out flat like a gigantic scythe had moved straight through. I struggled to focus my eyes on the strange, house-shaped object on the hill. It looked like a house and again it didn't. Mainly because where the roof should be there was nothing and the wall toward me was gone. The rooms stood open as you'd expect on a doll house. And then I knew — that was

the Snodhopper's house. A tornado must have hit.
Dumb old Diablo must have hooked us onto a
tornado . . . or was it dumb old me?

My head was hurting so, I couldn't think . . .
not clearly. Only somewhere I felt a warning sounding. I knew I had to get rid of my orange jump
suit, and I instinctively reached for the zipper. I
connected with shreds of my T-shirt. Very carefully I moved my eyes downward toward my chest.
My head wanted no sudden movements. There was
no bright orange anywhere. I tried to pull myself
to my feet and fell flat. After the lights stopped
flashing in my brain, I found out why. The orange
suit was in tatters around my feet. I worked the
bits and pieces off and slowly, carefully stood up
and turned toward the spot where our house should
be. But I was so scared that there might be nothing
there that I shut my eyes. Pretty stupid, yes? You
can't see much with your eyes shut.

I forced myself to look and what I managed was
more like a squint in the direction home should be.
There it was. I felt weak with relief. Now I moved
my eyes to the left and the emptiness hit me like
a blow. The barn was gone. Not a sign of it re-
mained. A thought skipped through my brain. The
barn's being totaled was logical. We'd brought a
tornado right to it. Or had the tornado brought us?
It was very confusing.

Which made me think of Diablo. I had to find

the horse. I don't know why this feeling surfaced, but it did. I was stumbling across the crushed corn stalks in the general direction of the missing barn when my toe caught on something hard. Carefully I looked down. I'd found Diablo's leg. Then I found another and another. I put them together like you do when you're working a puzzle. Each time I ranged a little farther and still farther. What I was doing didn't make sense, but I kept on at it. When you're hurt bad your mind doesn't work sensibly. I found the hindquarters with the saddle and the other leg. I was still missing the front parts.

I have no idea how long it took me to find the last bits and pieces. About forever it seemed. But

when I finally came across the head and lugged it back to the rest, I gave up. Everything was whirling. Another word or maybe idea was trying to escape from my buzzing brain. It was too much work to figure it out. I have no idea whether I lay down or fell down. I only know that everything was suddenly black.

Mom says that she and Dad were panicked when they returned from the airport and saw what havoc the tornado had wreaked. They were even more scared when the scientists told them that Julie and I were in the barn when it was hit. She can describe everyone's frantic search for us so vividly that it gives me goose pimples to hear it. And then

I have to laugh when she tells about their coming across me, lying on top of a wild assortment of carved wood and clutching in my arms the head of a mad-looking wooden horse. I was lying so still that they all thought I was dead.

Which, of course, I wasn't. But I did have one dandy skull fracture and that made things pretty awful for a few days. Mom reports that I said wild things while I was delirious: stuff like negative worlds and positive thinking and the value of telling the truth. How I begged Julie to tell me how to get the — she paused here trying to remember the word — transductor, that was it. She thought it such an odd word that she had looked it up in the dictionary, not really expecting to find it there. And when she found the meaning, she was puzzled that I should even know the word let alone be worried about using one. She kind of skipped over the weights. I suddenly knew that before I blacked out, that was the idea that had been trying to surface. My brain had been trying to warn me to find the weights and hide them. Good thing I hadn't looked. Because the scientists had searched everywhere and not located one of them.

Finally Mom got around to Julie. She was nervous as she talked about her. Upset because they had never found a trace of her. When I was first coming around, I remembered being asked about Julie. I stuck to the truth there. I always said she had gone home. And not to worry. They thought I meant she was dead. So they dragged the lake and even the river. They looked under every pile of debris, combed the woods, drained the ditches. There was nothing they left undone in the search. Made me feel silly to have them going to all that work when the kid wasn't even in our world. Not anymore. Which set me thinking and worrying about whether Julie had made it home. She'd been in bad shape. And the transmuter could have been damaged or too old . . . What if she got caught between two worlds? That thought scared me. Mom decided talking about Julie was holding back my recovery. From there on in, she avoided the subject.

And then Grandma came to visit. She was on crutches because of her hip, so she couldn't do much but sit. And I was in the same boat. Bones in one's skull take their time about healing. So the two of us sat and talked. We talked about Julie, lots about Julie. Grandma said you should talk out things that troubled you. Sounded like a good idea to me. I decided to give it a try. My words just tumbled out. Oh, I couldn't tell Grandma everything about Julie and our adventures, but I told her plenty. And she came to share my opinion that Julie was a very special person.

And then one day, Mom and Dad handed me about the biggest surprise I'd ever had. I could tell something was going on. Dad began spending hours in the basement, which wasn't a bit like him. I couldn't figure out what he was doing. Next thing I knew Mom was doing the same thing, working in the basement. It was crazy and lonesome too. Grandma and I spent our evenings now watching TV. Sometimes if I came in suddenly when the folks were talking, they'd stop their words in mid-stream. It was all mighty peculiar.

Yet with all this going on, I still didn't expect anything unusual the night Mom called me "to come and see something in the living room." I thought she probably wanted to show me a new blossom on her gardenia plant or surprise me with a big piece of cake. By now I'd lost so much weight that everyone kept urging me to eat. It's a crazy world, I was thinking as I walked in the door. For a minute I couldn't take in what my eyes were seeing, for right there in our bay window in all his wild, exciting madness was Diablo Grande. For a minute I didn't feel anything. Then flashes of delight, sheer undiluted delight shot through me. I couldn't say a word.

Mom thought my silence was anger, disapproval, maybe even disgust. "Oh, I am sorry. We didn't think. Oh, Simon, it reminds him of . . . of that awful day and the tornado."

I couldn't believe it. My tall, calm, matter-of-fact Mom was about to burst into tears. And here I was so darn happy I couldn't talk. I told you it was a crazy world. "Mom!" The word shot out of me. "Mom, it's Great . . . it's absolutely GREAT! That's Diablo. That's the wooden horse Julie and I found in our barn. How absolutely great."

I think my deep gladness came through. They knew I really felt what my words were saying and that all their efforts to surprise me had been worthwhile.

Grandma said, in a smug way, "I told you it was a good idea." And we all stood there grinning like idiots.

First thing I did was walk over and look at him, close up. He was the same Diablo. They'd done a great job in glueing him back together and redoing his paint job. His black color was blacker than ever . . . the saddle had wild happy colors running all over it . . . the tail looked like it might go into action at any minute. I reached up to unscrew the right ear. It was firmly stuck in place. Mom noticed my action.

"That ear was missing, Barney. How surprising you should notice. Dad had to carve a new one. Didn't he do a perfect job?"

He'd done a great job all right. But how enthusiastic can you get when you suddenly realize that from now on you're as earthbound as the next guy. Still I gave it my best, because I didn't want Dad to feel I was downgrading his carving of ears.

Then as I thought about it later I came to understand that anything the size of the transductor caught in a wind with the power of a tornado was gone for good. Nobody, but nobody, would ever find it again.

The next afternoon when everyone was busy at his own thing, I climbed up on Diablo's back. It felt natural . . . very familiar, a little tippy, maybe because the new stand wasn't as firm as the old one. Sitting there started me to dreaming, thinking about Julie and our trips and the things she used to talk about. Things like positive and negative worlds. Could two worlds really exist back to back, operating at the same time? Was it really possible that the people where she came from revered the truth and all living things, that they really let kids progress at their own speed through the levels of learning? Now that sounded like a great idea. But where did that leave us? Positive or negative? And how about positive thinking? It had really seemed to work. Which made me start thinking about whether I'd ever hear from Julie again. You can imagine how startled I was when Grandma's voice said, "Why, Barney . . ."

I hadn't even heard her come in. I felt awfully embarrassed, getting caught like that. I bet I looked pretty silly sitting on a merry-go-round horse as big as I am. I scrambled off in record time muttering something about, "just thinking."

"That's a wild-looking horse," said Grandma, hitching herself forward with her crutches.

"He and Julie were a lot alike," I said.

"You really think so?" asked Grandma. "I knew your parents called her wild, but you . . . ? I'm surprised."

"Julie was wild, Grandma. But not wild in the sense the folks mean. You know why I said she was like Diablo? Because they both wanted to be free. Diablo's fighting the bit . . . Julie was fighting to get home."

At that point I ran out of words. What did I think I was doing? If I kept on, Grandma was going to get very curious about some of my statements. I shut up.

But she didn't. Grandma had something else on her mind and she was anxious to get on with it. "I came hunting for you, Barney," she said, "because I found this poem." She held a book out toward me. "I don't understand why, but I knew I had to show it to you. It was almost as if someone were telling me 'show it to Barney.' It's rather ridiculous, isn't it? I've never known you to like poetry. And yet, I couldn't stop myself. So here it is."

Grandma had my reaction to poetry pegged exactly right. Dumb stuff. But I took the book, trying to be polite. Or maybe thinking about Julie had made me just a little bit kinder. Hey, could Julie be trying to reach back to me, to tell me something?

There was a thought to send excited shivers dancing in my stomach.

When I glanced at the poem, I gave a little sigh of relief. At least it was short. I read it through once . . . then again and again. Holy cow! A poet had actually made me understand my summer with Julie. He had caught the magic of it all. It's funny how I had to read and reread it over and over. In fact, I read it so often that I learned it by heart. Sometimes now I like to sit in the living room as I am now, looking at Diablo and saying part of the poem out loud. It makes Julie seem very close to me.

> Ride a wild horse
> against the sky
> hold tight to his wings . . .
>
> Before you die
> whatever else you leave undone,
> once, ride a wild horse
> into the sun.*

And I know, as I say those words, I know I am one of the lucky ones, for that summer that Julie came to stay, I rode a wild horse into the sun. It has made all the difference.

* "Ride a Wild Horse" by Hannah Kahn.